MAX AND THE
BANJO FERRET

Book Three of Max and the Multiverse

A novel by Zachry Wheeler

ISBN: 978-0-9982049-6-3
Edited by Jennifer Amon
ZachryWheeler.com

This stupid book is dedicated to the almighty Tim, the alpha and omega, yin and yang, regular and unleaded.

CHAPTER 1

Life takes an almost hedonistic pleasure in pointing out the things you don't know. Take peanuts, for instance. Nobody grew up knowing that they were legumes in disguise. And to this day, grown-ass adults will reach for antibiotics when they catch a cold.

And then there are the big ones.

Any nerd worth their weight in hexagonal dice knows about the four fundamental forces of nature: gravitational, electromagnetic, strong, and weak. However, very few know about the fifth. Yes, fifth. Much like its siblings, the fifth was created during the Great Booyah. (Earth humans call it the Big Bang because they refuse to accept galactic norms, like how Americans insist on using imperial units when the rest of the world uses metric.)

The fifth's signature force is that of a goading prick, the cosmic equivalent of a shit-stirring uncle at Thanksgiving. Its overall purpose is to keep the universe guessing. Sometimes it hides car keys or bluescreens a computer. Other times it inflames an interstellar war just to watch the pretty colors. The fifth is an embodiment of astronomic indifference. It just ruffles random feathers and skips away like an incorporeal Bill Murray prancing across the cosmos.

This was why Max sat upon a log with his face buried in his

hands. But not just any log. This log rested on the surface of Yankar, a lush jungle planet located in the Perseus-Pisces Supercluster. An unfortunate shift had stranded him there away from his crewmates, the result of a rousing party and subsequent pass out. A conundrum for sure, but Max didn't care much at the moment. He was too busy contemplating the most mind-bending nugget of information he had ever received, from his lifelong best friend no less.

There he sat, slumped and silent with nappy dreadlocks dangling from his head. A thick beard peeked through a set of muscular forearms. Stitched hides, strapped boots, and a claw necklace completed the image of a distraught caveman having lost his favorite rock.

Ross, currently a large and fearsome saber-toothed tiger, sat across from Max with his head tilted in mild concern. He glanced away and sighed as if to conjure a feckless pep talk, then returned his gaze to the caveman.

"Oi," Ross said. "You okay there, mate?"

Max's hands dropped to his knees with a limp slap. The sudden reveal of an angered face caught the tiger off-guard. Ross recoiled and cocked an ear back.

"This is hardly the time or place for one of your cruel jokes," Max said.

"Eh?" Ross cocked the other ear back.

"You've done this before. Hell, you've been yanking my chain since day one. Remember? Your real name is Reginald, first son of Asshole from the Assholian Galaxy?"

Ross smirked. "Oh yeah, that was a good one. First son of *Hackamore* from the *Zynfall* Galaxy. And mostly true, by the way. There was this crystal planet full of—"

"Stop. Just, stop." Max paused to take a needed breath. "You just told me, with a straight face no less, that you are the Fifth Force of Nature, that you were created during Big Ba—the Great Booyah, and that your role in the universe is to fuck with everyone."

Ross nodded.

Max rolled his eyes, palmed the log, and shot to his feet. He grabbed his spear and started to walk away. "I can't do this right now. I'm stranded on a planet full of giant horror monsters that want to eat my face. I need to gather my wits and figure out how to get back to Zoey and Perra."

"I can help with that."

"And how can you do that?" Max said without looking back or breaking stride.

"I know where they are and what they're doing. Right now. Across all universes."

Max stopped, huffed, and bowed his head. After a brief pause to digest the utter frustration of the predicament, he lifted his eyes and surveyed the open field. Waist-high grass swayed in the gentle breeze. Towering trees the size of office buildings lined the far side, shrouding the horizon. His gaze climbed the wooden wall to a blue sun peeking through the clouds. The orb blinked as a giant winged monstrosity sailed overhead. The flap of massive wings drowned out the forest. The creature shrieked, sending a chill down Max's spine. It banked and glided around the open basin, as if sensing the fear of an Earthling snack.

"We should probably get out of the valley," Ross said as he followed the plane-sized beast with widened eyes.

Max groaned, about-faced, and jogged back to the forest line. Ross spun around and leapt into a trot as Max passed. The pair slipped through a drapery of vines and vanished into the jungle.

* * *

On the far side of the universe, Zoey and Perra prepped their boxy freighter for launch after delivering lunch to an asteroid. But not just any lunch. This lunch had contained the roasted flank steak of a burkelbob, one of three known to exist. The creatures were prized for their delectable flesh and ultimate scarcity. They had no lungs, blood, or sensitivity to extreme cold, so they were perfectly content floating around the vacuum of space. Their origin and propagation remained a mystery. In fact, their entire existence was uncovered by a chance encounter. After all, one tends to remember when a space pig smiles at you from a port window.

Their extreme rarity dictated their extreme price point. Only the wealthiest beings in the universe could afford a burkelbob steak. We're talking the upper one quadrillionth of the upper one percent. A handful of individuals, four to be exact, one of which had purchased an entire star system in order to convert a prized asteroid into a vacation home. On this day, and in that very home, she joined one of the most exclusive clubs in all existence by tasting a burkelbob steak.

Zoey and Perra's ship rested atop a launch pad made of solid diamond. (Don't get too excited. Diamonds might be precious on Earth, but the universe at large is littered with them. In fact, there are entire planets made of diamond. As with most material goods, rarity and value are intertwined. When the exceedingly wealthy propose to their schmoopsie poos, it's not with a trashy diamond ring. They use a slice of dried burkelbob intestine.)

Inside the cockpit, the orange Mulgawats sulked inside their respective pilot seats. They stared out the viewport at a diamond staircase lifting from a diamond landing pad up to a diamond front door encrusted with more diamonds. Zoey rapped her fingers on the crescent control panel. Light pats and random blips needled an idle silence.

She sighed and rubbed her forehead. "I can't believe we just did that. 'Precious Cargo Delivery Service, here's your snack.' We may as well start delivering pizzas."

Perra maintained a blank stare out the viewport.

Zoey turned to her catatonic lover and waved a hand in front of her face. "You okay there, sweetie?"

Perra flinched in response. "Sorry. I just have a nagging feeling that we're forgetting something important."

"Like what? This was a one-way trip, no pick-up."

"No, nothing like that. Something raw and personal, like a missing limb."

Zoey glanced at her arms and legs, then felt moronic for doing so.

"Ah!" Perra leapt to her feet. "Forgot to lock down the engine room. Be right back."

Zoey smirked as Perra tromped down the corridor.

* * *

Max crept through the jungle foliage with spear at the ready and a large tiger in tow, as if playing an intense game of *Jumanji*. Every squawk and snap yanked his focus. Every flinch and flex stretched leather across his chest. His teeth started to chatter, much to the annoyance of Ross.

"Mind if I take point?" Ross said, then plodded ahead before Max could answer. "You're under the lower canopy now, no need to freak out. Most of the bigger beasts stick to the valleys and upper canopies."

Max softened his shoulders and relaxed a bit. He raised the tip of his spear overhead and used it as a walking stick. "Then why are you in here?"

"Mate, you watched a dinosaur the size of a building eat a spider the size of a bus. What makes you think that I'm a bigger beast on this planet?"

Max whimpered and re-gripped his spear.

"You're perfectly safe, though. Down here, I'm the King of the Jungle."

Max faltered and held his spear at kinda-ready, as if to say that he's sort of prepared for whatever, or something. He grunted, shook it off, and returned to the casual walk of a forest nomad. "So where are we going?"

"Your place."

"My place? I have a home here?"

"You have a tree house, in a manner of speaking, which is kind of a requirement. Primitive versions of Yankar aren't exactly hiker-friendly. At least, not for humans. You figured that out early on, else we wouldn't be chin wagging."

"See, that's what I don't understand. How did I—er, this version

5

of me, get here in the first place?"

"Infinite universes, infinite possibilities."

Max grimaced. "Okay, so I was flying around Earth on my jet-pack, impressing my supermodel girlfriend, when all the sudden, a portal to Yankar opened up and swallowed me like a fish."

"Yup."

Max raised an eyebrow. "Really?"

"In some universes, sure. But not in this one. You were abducted from Earth and dumped here, probably because of your incessant whinging."

"Whin—that's not a word."

"Whinging, as in 'to whinge.' To complain in a persistent and annoying way. Or as I shall call it from this day forth, 'Maxing.'"

"No need to be a dick."

"You mean a *Max*?"

Max rolled his eyes. "Or maybe you do. You are Dicky McDickerson after all, the Fifth Force of Nature." He added air quotes and a mocking tone. "So does that mean the real Ross is back on Earth being a normal house cat?"

"Yes, and I'm him too."

"Huh? How can you be him and you?"

Ross stopped and turned to Max. "I'm a Force of Nature, you twit. Just like gravity. I'm everywhere, at all times and through all universes. In fact, hold on a sec ..." Ross glanced away for a moment, then returned a cheeky grin. "I just shat in your gaming chair back on Earth."

Max grimaced and shook his head. "You really are a big hairy asshole."

"Kind of the point, mate. It's why I love being a house cat. I can break stuff, puke everywhere, howl in the middle of the night like a batshit banshee, and you still feed me. It's like a free pass for outright douchery."

"So every time you scratch the furniture or knock over a vase, it's just ..."

"Yup." Ross turned away and resumed his walk.

"Wow. That explains so much." Max paused in thought, then jogged to catch up. "I'm actually kind of impressed, to be honest."

"That's nothing. You should see me work on a planetary scale."

"How so?"

"Well, one of my favorite things to do is start religions in different regions and see how long it takes them to fight. I'll appear to some barmy schmuck on one side of a planet, then to another schmuck on the other side, then start the clock for a holy war. My record is 26 days."

"You mean to tell me that the Crusades, the Inquisition, all of them, were just ..."

"Yup."

"Unreal."

"No offense, but Earthlings are some of the most gullible knobs in the universe. Check it, I got piss drunk one day and decided to mess with some random wanker. I appeared to him as a giant purple banjo-playing ferret, called myself Tim the Destroyer of Worlds, and told him that I would destroy the Earth if humans didn't stop being so goddamn stupid. I thought for sure that he would dismiss me as some sort of hallucination. Nope. Two weeks later, boom! Ferretianism was born. It took less than a decade for it to spread across the galaxy. They have a governance hierarchy, missionary system, the whole enchilada."

Max thought for a moment. "That's why everyone uses *Tim* for curses and such."

"Exactly, and it remains one of my finest works, despite its imprudent creation. A universe-wide religion that traces its roots to an Earthling halfwit. They even have a website. You should check it out. It's as funny as it is depressing."

Max glanced at his leathery duds and spear. "Yeah, I'll get right on that."

Ross strolled to a stop at the base of a colossal tree. Max's jaw slacked open as he traced a tangled maze of vines up a giant bark wall, each as thick as his leg. He glanced left and right, unable to see the tree's curvature.

"You see the vine on the left?" Ross said. "The one with pegs sticking out of it?"

Max located the vine in question. An alternating pattern of crude wooden stakes protruded from its thick hide. "Yes, I see it."

"That's your home ladder. Just climb until it's obvious." Ross crouched, wiggled his bum, and leapt onto the wall of wood, sinking his giant claws into the bark. He climbed up the tree just like any normal feline and disappeared over a hidden ledge.

Max slipped his spear into a rear belt loop and lifted his gaze to the canopy far above. Dangling vines swayed in the breeze, creaking like trees themselves. Broad leaves the size of cars layered above one another. Beams of sunlight poked through the foliage with every gust of wind. Max drank in the vibrant visual and smiled. "You know, maybe this place isn't as bad as I thi—" A mystery screech yanked Max from his ponder. Every muscle in his body seized with an influx of panic. He sprinted over to the pegged vine and scrambled up the wall like a caffeinated rock climber. With a final grip and yank, he hurtled over a ledge and flopped onto his back, landing on a bed of spongy moss.

After a stint of heavy panting with a hand clasped to his chest, Max mustered the courage to peek over the ledge. The forest floor seemed clear, as best as he could tell. Just rocks, dirt, and a creepy critter that one might describe as a hulked out cockroach. Max scratched his beard and climbed to his feet, using the wall behind him as leverage. A slow scan of the immediate area uncovered a narrow ledge carved into the tree, similar to a switchback in a mountain pass. Curious eyes traced the path up to a bundle of dangling vines, bound together over a small hollow. Max scrunched his brow and stepped towards the entrance.

A gentle hook and pull revealed a cave-like area tucked inside the tree. Nothing substantial, just a simple alcove the size of a studio apartment. Slivers of sunlight fell from the knotted ceiling and into a collection of well-placed quartzes, illuminating the space with soft light. Max stepped inside and released his grip on the vines, leaving him to the peace and quiet of his own Yankar abode. It reeked of damp rot and body odor, not that Max could tell in his current state. Off to the side, a curled tiger rested on a bed of twigs and dried moss.

"So you live here too, then?" Max said.

"No," Ross said. "However, this is my territory."

"But I made you a bed."

"No, this is *your* bed. But it's in my territory, so it's *my* bed. Standard cat law."

Max shook his head and started to examine the hollow. A handful of stumpy logs served as a living room. A cubby in the wall housed a collection of crude tools ripped straight from the Stone Age. Max unhooked his spear and leaned it against a wall knot. Dirty fingers traced an array of carved images, rough stick figures of various animals, each with the standard happy face of a kindergarten art project.

Below them was a large rectangle chiseled into the wall, about a meter wide and floating above a stone base. A hunk of wood rested on top, resembling a warped shoebox. Max picked the block up and studied the markings etched onto the face. A pair of thin vines connected the box to V-shaped twigs resting on the ground. The realization hit Max like a wet fish across the face. He frowned, expelled a heavy sigh, and returned the block to its stony stand.

"That is the saddest and most pathetic thing I have ever seen in my entire life."

"Hmph?" Ross stirred on the mossy bed.

"It's a gaming console. Apparently, I was so distraught at losing it, that I needed to recreate the experience inside a dank tree hollow." He glanced down to a round depression in the floor. "I sit right here and stare at a blank wall while tapping sticks connected by vines to a block of wood. What the fuck is wrong with me?"

"Don't overthink it. It's the part of home you missed the most."

"Still, though. Shouldn't I have stick dolls of friends and family or something?"

Ross lifted his head to make eye contact. "Do you miss them?"

Max thought for a moment, but did not respond.

"There's your answer."

Max bowed his head and shuffled to the center of the room. He plunked his wearied body onto a log and sulked. Ross rose onto his front paws and stiffened his neck, as if to guard an Egyptian tomb for a moment. Max batted at one of the dreadlocks hanging in front of his face. He sighed and turned to Ross.

"I miss Zoey and Perra." Max scratched his beard and glanced around the hollow. "I miss the ship. I miss my bed. I miss the crisp, clean air."

"Don't forget hygiene."

Max raised an arm, sniffed his pit, and recoiled with a wide-eyed neck snap. "Yes, that too."

"So the question reveals itself. What are you going to do about it?"

Max shrugged. "Apart from shifting back to the Yarnwal party, I don't see what else I can do."

Ross raised his brow.

Max responded with a slow nod. "I need to shift back."

Ross raised his brow a little higher.

"Which means ... I need to fall asleep. A lot. Like, over and over until I get back."

"Bingo. And that's where I come in. While I am a Force of Nature, I cannot command nature. I can, however, exert some influence. I can zot your noggin, knock you out, and yank you back, as many times as it takes."

A hopeful smile stretched across Max's face.

"But, and this is a big but, it's going to feel like a street fight with Mike Tyson."

Max didn't flinch. "Let's do it."

"It may take hundreds, even thousands of tries, each of them feeling like a sledgehammer to the face."

Max leapt to his feet. "Don't care, I'm in!" He pumped his fists, but the giddiness deflated. "But, what if they don't remember me? What if I shift to a version where I started here and we never met?"

"Doesn't matter. All you need to do is find them, sneak into the ship, and get to space. Once you do, your domain will transfer back to the freighter and your shifts will reset. There are only so many ways an Earthling can hook up with a pair of Mulgawat couriers. I mean, I guess you could have brain-bonded with a robotic beaver and—"

"Couriers!" Max asserted so hard that his body bounced off the ground. "They're couriers! You can appear to them and tell them to come pick me up!"

Ross raised an eyebrow. "Hi there. I'm the Fifth Force of Nature. Yes, fifth, the one who loosens all the nuts and bolts in the engine room. Anyhoo, there's a stranded Earthling on a jungle planet millions of light-years away. You don't know or care about him in any way, but you need to go pick him up, for reasons. It will take weeks to get there and you need to hurry. It's all for naught if he falls asleep."

Max groaned and plunked back onto the log.

"First things first. Let's get you off of Yankar."

CHAPTER 2

The Terramesh was a cluster of stolen planets. Eighty-six to be exact, all bound together by enormous sky bridges. The colossal structure resembled an atomic molecule floating in the blackness of space, the same model adorning the desks of every high school science teacher. The manacled mass floated around a red hypergiant in the Milky Way Galaxy. Earth scientists called the star VY Canis Majoris, a decidedly unsexy name for something a billion times bigger than the sun. Locals called the star Behemet, and truth be told, that wasn't very good either.

Long ago, Behemet was home to 37 different planets, all with their own traits and orbital cycles. However, due to the star's immense size, the planets weren't technically planets. They were outer belt worlds similar to Pluto and Ceres. Any normal planets that managed to form around Behemet had long since perished. Or rather, disintegrated inside a raging nuclear inferno. The remaining outer worlds were small and rocky, similar in size to Earth. One of them even managed to spawn complex life. After a rousing period of evolution, its scientists unlocked the mysteries of spaceflight and decided to terraform the other planets. Before long, a multi-world civilization rooted into the solar system.

For thousands of years, citizens traveled back and forth between the worlds of their choosing. Climates spanned the spectrum, everything from warm and populous to cold and desolate. Cityscapes filled the temperate planets, attracting big business and eager youngsters. The outer planets offered peace and seclusion, attracting retirees and fringe lunatics. And for the brave few who favored the outer reaches, they could purchase land by simply pointing at it, because no one in their right mind would ever want to live there.

Wealthy citizens traveled the gamut, including a young corporate executive named Isella. She loved the hustle and bustle of the big city planets, but also longed for the frigid tranquility of the outer worlds. As a very successful businesswoman, she maintained a presence on multiple planets. But when time came to relax, she retreated to one of her many vacation homes in the outer belt. And thanks to a hyperline transport system, she was able to travel back and forth with relative ease. Shuttle commutes took several days (or a few weeks depending on planetary alignments), but the serenity was always worth the hassle.

Isella owned a company that experimented with holistic gravitational manipulation, a fancy way of saying *fun with gravity*. It started off as a scientific organization with a focus on improving space travel, but quickly shifted into a profit model when they developed a weight loss pill that actually worked. In lieu of reducing actual mass, they created tiny anti-gravity fields inside fatty tissue, reducing weight on a technicality. They sold like hotcakes (well, more like warm fumbungers) and made Isella a very rich woman. The tidal wave of sudden wealth taught her a valuable lesson: never underestimate people's willingness to bullshit themselves.

Infused with an immense fortune, Isella started to focus on what every affluent citizen does: herself. She dismissed the needs of the many in order to address the problems that affect her own slice of the opulent pie. Her primary gripe was the commute between planets, which took far too long for her own tastes. With the leverage of enormous wealth, she set out to shorten her commute by any means necessary. Localized jumps were illegal under Federation law, so that was out. She thought about lobbying to change the law, but she would be long dead before that bureaucratic slog came to an end. Teleportation was a pipedream fantasy (at least, to anyone outside of the Suth'ra Society).

But then she got a nutty idea.

While sipping on an expensive scotch at her penthouse desk, Isella came to the realization that her focus was wrong. She couldn't shorten the commute, but she *could*, in theory, shorten the distance. (It would help to point out that any reasonable person could simply relocate to a better system or buy a climatized moon, but as history has shown us time and time again, excessive wealth renders people far from reasonable.) She did own a gravitational diet company after all, so her idea carried some merit.

The plan was simple: tether planets with a concentrated gravity lock and reel them closer together. The governing council scoffed at her ridiculous proposal, but reconsidered after she wheeled barrels of money into the chamber.

It took well over a decade to iron out the kinks. After a few city destructions and moon collisions (not to mention a slew of PR hassles tied to the mass casualties), she managed to perfect the process. Isella tethered the first two planets within 50,000 miles of each other, then started work on a permanent atmo-bridge. Well, *started work* would be a tad generous. She gave canned speeches to shareholders while millions of underpaid workers risked their lives to connect two giant rocks with some metal rope. Years later, Isella cut the ribbon on a gleaming sky bridge, complete with high-speed mag-trams. The two planets were officially locked in a gravitational dance, floating around the belt like a makeshift dumbbell. The methods for maintaining orbital equilibrium remained a guarded company secret.

Fresh off the monumental success, Isella green-lighted the next planet. And the next, and the next, on and on until every belt planet was connected via a tangled web of steel. After trillions of credits, billions of work hours, and millions of deaths, Isella finally had an acceptable commute.

She enjoyed it ... for a time.

Isella realized far too late that being close to everything meant that she was close to *everything*. She couldn't escape anymore. Going to her vacation home meant staring at her office planet in the sky. She yearned for the sweet serenity of isolation. Thus, she started purchasing properties on other planets in nearby solar systems. It was delightful, until she tired of the commute.

The nutty idea returned, this time with the delusional insanity of a criminal mastermind. She started "collecting" planets like a hoarder collecting knick-knacks. She spent an untold fortune developing plunder tech, where a monstrous stealth vessel bored itself into an unsuspecting planet, spun a jump drive the size of a small town, and blinked the entire world to the Behemet system. Isella managed to steal every rocky planet in Canis Major before the Federation of Planets intervened. She spent the rest of her life in a small concrete cell, broke but happy.

The collapse of her mighty enterprise also collapsed the Terramesh economy. In the end, 86 planets went bankrupt all at once, sparking the single greatest economic disaster in the history of the universe. It never recovered. Most of the inhabitants fled. Thousands of years later, the mesh housed anyone that dared to traverse it. It turned into a haven for criminals, deviants, and televangelists. Some worlds offered lavish casinos with upscale brothels and seedy underbellies, like Las Vegas on a cosmic scale. Other worlds embraced their criminality and served as harbors for organized raider factions, like Las Vegas on a cosmic scale.

In recent days, the Terramesh was home to numerous clans, including the Navcarks, Dread Jacks, and Moreons. The core planets once housed the fearsome Varokins, but a massacre at Hollow Hold depleted their fleet. The Moreons had since taken control.

Jarovy, the innermost planet, was Isella's homeworld and the first bound to another. It was a commerce center before the mesh, but had since grown into a metal-plated monstrosity. Every square mile of its surface was covered by steel and concrete. Skyscrapers stretched from pole to pole, transforming the planet into a perpetual cityscape. It stood out as the only world inside the cluster without a view of space. The surfaces of its bound neighbors filled every sliver of sky. It also featured the most bridges, connecting to every nearby world like a silvery sea urchin. In a very real sense, it served as the beating heart of the Terramesh.

*   *   *

A black service shuttle sailed through the chaotic space between planets, carving through traffic with the confidence of a helmetless jackass on a crotch rocket. It zipped under a gleaming sky bridge several miles in diameter, its shadowy hull reflecting off the sheen. The colossal pillar connected a snowy world on the left to a desert planet on the right. The shuttle crested a final planet to bring a metallic globe into view. Jarovy pulsed at the center of the Terramesh, its vast steel tentacles plunging into neighboring worlds. Countless vessels filled the void, everything from raider fleets to battlecruisers. Jarovy breathed with nonstop activity. The entire surface glowed with the deep greens of artificial light.

The shuttle sliced through the atmosphere and fell into the jagged cityscape. It slipped between tarnished towers as it pushed towards a black monolith in the distance. The ship slowed to a hover and came to a rest upon a landing pad near the tower's peak. Metal claws gripped the surface as a ramp lowered from its base, coughing puffs of steam. Five figures in black robes emerged from the vessel and glided towards a large entrance door. The leader took point with the other four following in pairs. They came to a stop at the door, prompting the bulky plane to unlatch and slide open. The whine of neglected gears needled the ears of everyone present. The door clanked to a rest, revealing a beefy bloke with leafy green skin and cropped yellow hair leaning on the wall inside. Jai Ferenhal adjusted the tie on his tailored suit and turned his sapphire blue eyes to the visitors.

"Welcome back, m'lord," he said in a graveled voice.

The figure lowered its hood, unveiling the teardrop skull and purple skin of Lord Essien, commander of the Varokin forces. Her silvery eyes burrowed into the brute. "Jai."

"Were you followed?"

She narrowed her gaze.

"Sorry, force of habit." Jai cleared his throat and lifted from the wall. "Word on the wire is that Nifan knows you're here."

"So? Bitch is welcome to set foot on the mesh. Hell, even the dregs would take immense pleasure in cutting down The Dossier."

"Even so, our power has been greatly diminished here."

Essien took a step forward. "*Our* power?"

"The Varokins." Jai responded with a wide-eyed snap, then stammered like a child with his hand in the cookie jar. "The *collective* our, if you will."

"Last time I checked," Essien said, taking another step, "*you* are not a Varokin."

"I meant no disrespect, m'lord. I, um ..." Jai huffed and slouched. "Just scold me and get it over with."

Essien grinned and punched him in the shoulder. "I do miss fucking with you, Jai. Never disappoints."

"Um, thank you?"

Essien glanced at the minions behind her. "See? He even thanks me for it."

The posse snickered like cartoon villains.

"Anyway, let's get on with this shit show."

"This way, m'lord." Jai swung an open hand into the dark corridor.

Lord Essien stepped inside and floated down the tunnel with Jai tromping alongside. The interior of the Varokin headquarters (well, former headquarters) radiated darkness for the sake of darkness. Every nook, knob, and surface fell somewhere between charcoal and Batman. Even the lighting units glowed under panes of smoky glass. One half-expected to glance down a corridor and see Ripley doing battle with a xenomorph. Jai and Lord Essien rounded a corner with the four robed Varokins floating behind. Jai's weighted steps echoed down the tunnel as Essien and her minions glided in silence.

"Can you walk any louder?" Essien said.

Jai stammered and glanced down to his feet. His pricy dress shoes had wooden soles, which clanked on the grated metal like clogs on a dance floor. He stiffened his legs and shuffled for a while, trading clanks for scuffs, but his mind struggled to abide the diminishing value of his kicks. With dignity now a luxury, he decided to tiptoe like a Scooby-Doo villain.

Essien laughed. "Tim help me, you are such a dork."

Jai grunted and resumed his normal stride.

Essien wiped her eyes and punched him in the shoulder again. "Okay, so, give me the rundown on these morons."

"Moreons. Eon, like an era."

"Mor—oh, I totally heard that wrong."

"They manned a small outpost on Jarovy before seizing control of the Varokin strongholds. In fact, they maintained presences on all 86 planets inside the Terramesh. Most were housed in the temple colonies of Kurm, Hyoma, and Lovaka. The mesh largely dismissed them as religious kooks, just a bunch of irritating yet harmless missionaries. But, they used that facade to amass an armada right under our noses. They mobilized after the Hollow Hold defeat and conquered the mesh before anyone knew what had happened."

"Do I detect a hint of admiration?"

"Just impressed by the efficiency."

Essien sighed. "So a faction of holy fucknuts usurped the Varokins. I would rather deal with the Dread Jacks. At least they're reasonable between murders."

"Plus they have good coffee."

Essien nodded. "So what's the Moreon shtick? Sacrificial loons? Another sect of ferret worship?"

Jai chuckled. "No, nothing like that. But I should warn you that their beliefs are rather untethered."

"What religion isn't?"

"No, seriously. They're another Qarakish cult."

Essien huffed and shook her head. "Great. Just give me the highlights then."

"Well, speaking of good coffee, they don't drink any. Or alcohol.

Or flimgarbles. Standard purity complex. If it's fun in any way, they abstain."

"Any prophets?"

"Just one, some fishmonger named Joe. They believe he started the religion by talking to fish in a bucket. And I wish I were joking. There is something about golden tubas, plus all the classics like sanctioned racism and sexism. Oh, and they all wear magic t-shirts."

Essien snort-laughed.

"It's just a regular poly blend, but they treat it like a sort of spiritual armor. They actually believe that it will protect them from physical harm."

"Oh, this is going to be fun."

"The controlling faction is made up of Dimathiens, a race known for their pasty white skin and warped skulls."

"Warped?"

"Random, no rhyme or reason, like giant tumors with eyeballs."

"Ah."

"The leader's name is Trevor. He can be, um, artfully wholesome."

"Explain."

"He'll backstab you, but he won't cuss."

They rounded a final corner and into a cavernous foyer. Jagged metal panes adorned the walls and climbed to the peak of a vaulted ceiling, like the scaly insides of a dragon belly. Rows of sconces lined the walls, their lights flickering behind bubbles of clouded glass. A pair of towering steel doors veiled the nerve center of the Varokin headquarters. Two masked figures in ivory robes guarded the entrance, serving as a stark contrast to the grim surroundings. Lord Essien smirked as her posse approached.

* * *

Zoey and Perra's tiny freighter sailed along the outskirts of Xawynda, a dense galaxy located deep inside the Coma Cluster. They had visited a popular spa planet known for its combative take on relaxation. A peculiar humanoid species inhabited the world. Resembling deformed gremlins, they derived orgasmic pleasure from what most beings would consider immense pain. The harder the beating, the greater the climax, like achieving gratification by picking fights at biker bars. Once the species joined the Federation, it didn't take long for a crafty entrepreneur to monetize the activity. For a modest fee, visitors could beat the stuffing out of any local resident, then relax at a mineral hot spring. An ideal vacation spot for anyone needing to vent some bottled-up frustration. Perks included group hunts, role-playing, and a wide selection of blunt instruments.

After a delightful day of violent rejuvenation, Zoey and Perra set a course for a nearby system that housed a large PCDS outpost. With a glut of snacks and time to spare, they decided to build some momentum and cruise for a while. The autopilot took over, content to guide the ship through open space (i.e. go straight and try not to hit any planets). The ladies melted into their pilot seats with limp necks and lazy stares, as if to digest a massive dinner. Zoey lifted her fist and examined her reddened knuckles.

"I so needed that," she said.

Perra responded with a slow nod. "Mhmm."

"You know, the Earthlings say that laughter is the best medicine. I humbly disagree. Violence without consequence is a far superior tonic."

"I really liked my guy. His name was Narbulio, such a sweetheart. He even helped me with my uppercut between sessions. I'm going to ask for him next time."

Zoey chuckled. "I don't even remember my lady's name. I was in the zone, beat that mother to a pulp. Literal mother. Her younglings watched and cheered the whole time. It was like having my own little grandstand." She expelled a heavy sigh. "So satisfying."

Perra rolled her head towards Zoey. "So how long do we have until—"

A sudden thunk jostled the ship, forcing them to flinch and grab their armrests. The ship creaked and whined as a red energy field crawled across the viewport, infecting the cockpit with a crimson glow. Zoey and Perra leapt to their feet and stumbled for balance. The console powered down, leaving only the coms and life support online. Zoey swiped and tapped the control panel, but it refused to respond.

"What the hell?"

"We're still breathing," Perra said while eyeing the atmo levels. "No collision or structural compromise." She turned a troubled gaze to Zoey. "We've been disabled."

Zoey mirrored her concern, prompting Perra to spin into the corridor and sprint towards the engine room. She sailed through the cargo bay and slapped a wall panel on the far side, opening the maintenance shaft. Widened eyes scanned a dim interior full of pipes, wires, and components. A swift hand nabbed a flashlight from a nearby cubby. She hurried over to the main engine compartment and started scanning for damage or malfunctions.

"Everything is intact and functional," she said to Zoey, now standing in the doorway. Perra's gaze darted around the engine housing. "No fries, no shreds, nothing. We're still at full capacity."

"Alive, disabled, no damage."

Perra turned to Zoey. "Anchor field."

Zoey nodded. "Somebody wants to chat."

Outside, a glowing red cocoon surrounded the freighter. A hazy red beam tethered the bubble to the base of a large stealth cruiser. Its jet black hull blended into a backdrop of space, creating a triangular blot in a sea of stars. The vessel, over 50 times the length of the freighter, loomed as a lifeless specter. The crimson glow of the anchor beam reflected off a tinted viewport, shrouding its mysterious occupants. The beam shortened at a steady pace, drawing its prey into the jaws of a loading dock.

Back inside the freighter, Zoey plucked a pair of plasma pistols from a locker and tossed one to Perra. Their shared silence lifted an air of anxiety. Another loud thunk echoed through the ship as the stealth vessel locked them inside its belly. The ladies stood side by side in the center of the cargo bay with mirrored combat stances, eyeing the airlock door with a sharp intensity.

"Steady bursts until we secure the hangar," Zoey said. "Cover me from inside until I motion otherwise."

"Got it."

They raised their pistols to the door.

A nervous silence infected the room.

Soon after, the crackle of an incoming transmission filled the cargo bay.

"Oh, my lovelies," said the voice of a classy mistress. "I find it painfully amusing that you think you can blast your way out of this."

Perra's jaw slacked open and she lowered her pistol.

Zoey closed her eyes, bowed her head, and lowered her pistol as well.

The hologram figure of Orantha Nifan coalesced inside the cargo bay. She stood directly in front of Zoey and Perra as if to exchange pleasantries. Her signature silken robe hung from her shoulders and flowed down to her feet, creating a small pile of fabric on the floor. An ornate scarf concealed her neck and brow, leaving her ashen cheeks and cobalt eyes exposed.

Nifan smirked. "Hello, ladies."

CHAPTER 3

Max and Ross faced each other inside the tree hollow. Max sat upon a living room log with his legs crossed and posture attentive, as if to summon his best impression of a kung fu master. Ross sat on the floor a few feet away, staring back at Max with a slight head tilt. His gaze listed off to the side, prompting Max to follow in confusion. Ross lifted his meaty paw and started grooming his forearm. Max glanced around the room as if he had missed a cue. He returned a miffed gaze to the feline and cleared his throat.

Ross snapped to attention. "Right, sorry."

Max rolled his eyes.

"Okay, so, here's what's going to happen. I'm going to kill the lights in your coconut with a jolt of ... well, let's just call it energy."

Max raised an eyebrow.

"You're going to pass out, then I'm going to revive you with ... more energy."

Max raised the other eyebrow.

"I have positioned myself in all other universes in direct accord with your current location. Depending on where you shift, I may need some extra time to revive you properly. If you awake by yourself, don't just talk to any random beast thinking it's me. I'd hate to go to all this bloody trouble, only to have you swallowed by your own stupidity."

"What do you mean *where* I shift? Won't I be here?"

"Ideally, yes."

"That sounds far from ideal."

"Given the nature of your presence on Yankar, you will likely remain here in the tree. But, the entire planet is your current domain. In another universe, you may be leading a tribe of frog-faced cannibals on another continent."

Max puckered with concern.

"But don't worry, I'm on it. Just keep your cool until I find you. Don't do anything, don't talk to anyone, and if you find yourself in a precarious situation, just fake it until you make it ... or until you die a painful death."

Max frowned and twitched an eyelid.

"You ready?"

Max closed his eyes and took a few deep breaths. After a bout of terrifying contemplation, his eyelids opened, his gaze hardened, and he responded with a resolute nod.

Ross grinned as he reared onto his hind legs and pressed his paws together, striking a kung fu pose of his own. The image charmed Max as a sight to behold, as if plucked from the pages of an anthropomorphic comic. The saber-toothed cat stood with broad shoulders, orange stripes, and brushes of white fur akin to an aging mobster. The soft light reflected off his two large fangs, giving him a fearsome presence. Ross mimicked a feisty crane, indulged in a quick *wax-on-wax-off*, then punched Max in the face.

* * *

Lord Essien and her posse strolled to a stop in front of two masked guards in ivory robes. The towering steel doors behind them, previously unadorned, now featured a large silhouette of a man playing a tuba, painted white as a stark contrast to the ebon surroundings. The guards crossed a pair of spears in front of the entrance, drawing an eye roll from Lord Essien. Jai crossed his arms and glared at the Moreon men (a safe assumption despite the masks and robes).

"Lord Essien here to speak with Trevor," Jai said.

"Greetings, kind traveler. State your purpose."

Jai shifted his lips, glanced at Essien, then returned to the guards. "I just did."

The guards, utterly unprepared for such a brazen breach of protocol, stammered a bit before huddling in front of the doors for an emergency meeting. Whispers elevated as their gazes darted back and forth between the visitors and each other. Their hurried hands and frantic gestures told Lord Essien everything she needed to know. Noobs, and bad ones at that. With a final grunt and nod, the guards resumed their positions. They crossed spears again, albeit in a clumsy and uneven manner. Jai tilted his head, as if trying to find the funny in a bad improv sketch.

"Very well. You may proceed."

An awkward silence gripped the group.

Essien rolled her eyes, then cleared her throat.

"Oh, right," a guard said. He spun to an adjacent wall, tapped a code into a control panel, got it wrong twice, took his time on the third, then resumed a threatening stance that lost any and all threat.

The doors slid open with a steady whine, revealing the glow of a large white (previously black) room. Lord Essien squinted and recoiled, as if emerging from a mineshaft into daylight. The group proceeded inside, each eyeing a guard with a mixture of pity and contempt. Essien glanced around the circular enclosure, the base of Varokin operations for the last hundred years. Soaring walls housed various consoles and hologram touch screens. A group of Dimathien men in ivory robes manned each station. They ignored the visitors, content to tap and swipe as commanded. In the center, an angular throne sat upon an elevated platform. Its occupant, a white humanoid male in a white robe, arose to address the group. (Like, really white. The kind of white that makes an albino look like a Brazilian bikini model.)

"Greetings, Lord Essien," Trevor said with the voice of an effeminate hipster. He added a meager bow.

"Greetings, Fuckface Von Shit Stealer." Essien added a mocking curtsey.

The entire room flinched and turned cringing faces to the visitors.

Trevor shivered. "No need for foul language. You are a guest here."

"A guest in my own fucking home?"

The operators tightened their cringes.

"Language," Trevor said with the uptick of an irritated parent. "This is our home now. As I recall, your defeat at Hollow Hold was absolute."

"I wouldn't be standing here if that were the case."

"Yes, about that ..." Trevor folded his hands like a pious bishop. He lifted his lumpy noggin and studied Lord Essien through a pair of lopsided red eyes. "Why do you request a conclave with the Moreons?"

"My armada was destroyed. I need a new one."

"And how is that of my concern?"

"You have one. I want it."

Trevor chortled like a creepy weirdo who never learned to laugh like a normal person. "And why would I relinquish control of a fleet that managed to conquer Jarovy?"

"First off, you didn't *conquer* anything. You just moved in while I was away, like a filthy squatter tribe. Second, we both want the same thing."

Trevor lifted his brow, or whatever mound of face flesh constituted a brow. "Which is?"

"Control of the Terramesh, the most powerful criminal syndicate in the universe. The Varokins held it for a hundred years before you stole it like some power-hungry babysitter. How long do you think it will take the Dread Jacks to mount a full invasion? They fear the Varokins, not you. I know how to run it, how to manipulate it, how to squeeze it for power and resources. You *need* me. And as much as it pains me to admit, I need your fleet to hold it."

Trevor stroked a chin-like knob at the base of his skull, trying to convey villainous contemplation, but resembled a cartoon caricature. A tattoo of *holy shit she's right* across his forehead would have been more subtle. "Hmm, an alluring proposition, madam. I shall consider this partnership under one condition."

Essien folded her arms.

"You must convert to Moreonism."

Essien snorted and smirked.

"I'm dead serious."

"Oh, I know you are, which is why I find it funny."

Essien started to wander around the front of the room. She shed her cloak and let it fall to the ground, unveiling a tempered leather suit with riveted pauldrons connected by link and chain. The other four Varokins lowered their hoods, revealing their silver eyes, sunken cheeks, and dark purple skin. Jai stood his ground with a hardened expression and hands locked behind his back. Essien traded glances with the dozen robed minions staring back at her through glassy red eyes. She stopped in front of the central platform and glared up at Trevor.

"Why aren't any of you armed?" she said.

"Moreons prefer a nonviolent approach."

"Yet you built an armada."

"An effective intimidation tactic."

"A weapon unused is a useless weapon."

Trevor narrowed his eyes. "Rest assured, Varokin. Self-defense is not discordant with the Moreon faith."

"And yet, none of you are carrying weapons."

"Did you not ... where is this going?"

Essien grinned. "Zwaq, open base cove three."

"Yes, Master," a metallic voice said.

A floor panel behind Lord Essien slid open, prompting a rack of plasma weapons to rise from a hidden compartment. Jai and the four Varokins plucked rifles from the rack. They spread out around the room, causing the minions to squirm and trade worried glances. Lord Essien turned and plucked a plasma pistol from the rack.

"Zwaq, reset and lockdown command."

"Yes, Master."

The rack disappeared into the floor. The entrance doors bolted shut, sealing the guards outside. The muted thumps of frantic fists elevated a sense of dread. Every station froze and reset with the Varokin emblem, a serpent-like creature slithering through the eye socket of a teardrop skull.

Trevor's vacant expression morphed into the jolly *aha* of realization. "Oooh, everything is voice-controlled."

Essien rolled her eyes.

"Zwaq," Trevor said. "Get me a water with lemon."

Silence responded.

"It only responds to me, you dolt."

Trevor sighed and glared at Essien. "I would appreciate some latitude, missy. This is our first usurpation and we are still learning."

Lord Essien huffed and shook her head as she sauntered over to the nearest minion with a plasma pistol in hand. She armed the weapon, causing the minion to pucker his face. Without breaking stride, Essien grabbed an arm and yanked him to his feet, drawing a yelp of fright. She spun to his back, locked his wrist, and jammed the gun barrel under his knobby chin. The minion whimpered as Lord Essien turned her gaze to Trevor and smiled.

"So, dazzle me with your Moreon pitch."

Trevor shifted his lips, then took a deep breath. "Okay, so, Moreonism is—"

BLAM! The blast from Essien's pistol echoed around the chamber. Trevor and his minions flinched and cowered for cover. Jai and the Varokins stood their ground, unmoved by the blast. A spatter of oily green blood covered the console, the floor around it, and Lord Essien herself. She released the headless body, allowing it to smack the floor. Blood oozed from the neck hole, forming a large puddle. Essien strolled over to the adjacent console and grabbed the next minion. A stiff yank brought him to his feet. Essien jammed the barrel into his back and returned her gaze to Trevor.

"Go on," she said, smiling through a bloodied face.

Trevor regained some of his floundering composure and took another deep breath. "As I was saying, Moreonism is a faith that—"

"Is this one wearing a magic t-shirt?"

Trevor stammered. "Um, yes, all adherents are required to don the holy garm—"

BLAM! BLAM! BLAM! BLAM! Rapid shots burst through the minion's chest, painting the floor with flesh and blood. Trevor and the minions flinched and cowered again. Essien released her grip, allowing the twitching victim to smack the ground in front of her.

"Didn't work," Essien said.

A shaking Trevor returned to his feet. "Well, it's more of a spiritual armor than—"

BLAM! Essien killed the next minion with a single shot to the chest while maintaining eye contact with Trevor.

Trevor lifted a finger and opened his mouth.

BLAM! The next minion took a shot to the face, spraying his station with brain goo.

Trevor tried again, but stammered like a malfunctioning Jeff Goldblum.

Lord Essien sauntered around the chamber with pistol outstretched. "There!" *BLAM!* "Are!" *BLAM!* "No!" *BLAM!* "Gods!" *BLAM!* "Stop!" *BLAM!* "Being!" *BLAM!* "Stupid!" *BLAM!* Leaving the final minion alive, Essien loomed over him as green blood dripped from her face. She nodded to Jai and the Varokins, who aimed their rifles at Trevor upon the platform.

Trevor took a step back. "Wha—what are you doing?"

"Testing your faith." Essien dropped the pistol into the minion's lap. "Kill yourself."

A puzzled gaze responded. "Um ... what?"

"Eat the barrel of that pistol and pull the trigger. Or, we kill your dear leader."

"No!" Trevor said. "Suicide is a grave sin, Borren."

Borren shrugged and grabbed the pistol. "Well, yeah, but only if it's the one true death, right?"

Trevor nodded. "In theory, sure, but it's still a dice roll."

Essien scrunched her brow.

Jai and the Varokins traded confused glances.

Borren sighed with the same mental weight of choosing between candy bars. "Meh, I like my chances. And besides, I wouldn't want to dirty your duds. We have already racked up a nasty tailoring bill in here, am I right?"

Trevor laughed. "Very true, brother. Okay then, I trust your judgment."

Borren opened his mouth, pressed the barrel to the roof, smiled, and pulled the trigger. The blast exploded his head, raining blood and brains all over Essien and the console. His headless body sank into the chair with arms dangling off to the sides.

Lord Essien scooped the smoking pistol from his blood-soaked lap and turned a bewildered gaze to Trevor. "What the hell just happened?"

"Oh, Borren was doing me a solid. Good tailors on the Terramesh are hard to find. I just got these robes last week, so he was being courteous."

A hunk of brain resting on Essien's shoulder started to wiggle. It rolled off her leather suit and fell to the floor with a wet splat. Drops of blood leapt from her body and formed a small puddle. It broke away and slithered towards the first victim like a liquid Terminator. Bits of brain rolled, flopped, and wriggled towards their owner. Each piece crawled into the lifeless body and assumed its natural position. With a final slurp of green ooze, the reassembled body began to stir. Soon after, the remaining blood and guts around the room started to crawl toward their owners.

Lord Essien gnashed her teeth and stomped over to Jai. He managed to gulp before she buried a fist into his cheek. The impact launched him off his feet and thumped his back to the floor. Essien loomed over him, writhing and panting. "Dimathiens can regenerate?! Did you forget to mention that tiny yet wholly important detail?!"

"I, um—"

Essien jammed her pistol into his eye socket. "I know *your* sack-of-shit species can't regenerate. Give me a reason. Give me one, sweet, delectable, goddamn reason."

Jai trembled and clenched his mouth shut.

"Hey, hey, hey," Trevor said with open palms. "There is no need for violence here." He stepped over to the platform ledge and took a seat, bringing him to eye level. "We can die just like anyone else, but it takes us several tries. We are all born with a death allowance, a number of times we can bite the big one before we actually do. No one knows their tab. Sometimes it's ten, sometimes a hundred, a thousand. Hell, there was one of us that managed to die 26 thousand times before he actually did. It was marvelous. They even made it into a pay-per-view event."

Essien unplugged her pistol from Jai's peeper, tightened her posture, and wandered over to Trevor. Her furious gaze softened to one of utter stupefaction. She spread her arms into the universal *this makes no goddamn sense* pose. "Then why are you religious?"

Trevor started to respond, but caught himself.

"Your species has negated the entire reason why mortals bullshit themselves into thinking there is life after death. If you can take a blast to the face and shake it off like a stubbed toe, then what's the point?"

Trevor paused for thought. "Well, um, if we live good Moreon lives, then we get to rule our own spirit planets after we die. That's kinda cool."

"You rule your own planet *now*. Hell, you rule a planet that governs an entangled mesh of other planets."

Trevor paused for thought again. He started to respond, but stopped. He started to respond again, but stopped. His brain locked itself into a vicious loop of *this is neat, but wait a minute.*

"Lord Ess—" Jai said from the floor, only to stare down the barrel of Essien's pistol again. He flinched and sniveled. "If I may, the regen powers of the Dimathiens make them formidable allies. Reimagine the Hollow Hold assault, only this time with an army of invincibles. We may finally have the means in which to defeat Nifan."

Essien narrowed her eyes. "*We?*"

Jai groaned and flopped on the floor. "Goddamnit."

"Blasphemy!" Trevor said with a knee-jerk reaction.

"Gosh darn it all to heck!" a minion said.

Everyone turned to the second victim, now poking his fingers through the holes in his robe.

"My sincere apologies for the coarse language, but look at this. I need a new hallowed v-neck *and* new robes. Ugh, this is going to cost me a fortune." The minion stomped over to Lord Essien and poked her chest. "Now listen here, you trigger-happy tart. You owe me a set of shiny new robes and you best pay—"

BLAM! Essien shot him in the face.

CHAPTER 4

Max awoke inside a washing machine. Or rather, that's the impression his brain gave him when his eyelids opened. A pair of furry paws had grasped his shoulders and shook him like a ragdoll. The room spun, jerked, and twisted before the reality of the situation dawned on him. He flailed his arms, causing the paws to release their grip. Max's body plopped onto the ground, jolting an already throbbing headache. He leaned forward, rubbed his eyes, and blinked the tree cave into focus.

"Oi, you awake?" Ross said.

Max turned towards the voice and studied the large tiger in front of him. "You punched me in the face, asshole."

"Yes."

Max gripped the sides of his head and tried to steady the spinning room. "Did, um ... did you just shake me awake?"

"Yes."

"What the hell, man?! I thought you were going to use some sort of energy thing."

"That *was* the energy thing."

Max glared at the feline, then decided that the squabble wasn't worth the additional headache. "Did it work?"

"Yup."

Max perked up before realizing that he was still a dirty caveman with a scruffy beard.

"No dice on the Yarnwal, though. You're on a version of Yankar where ferns grow upside down."

Max deflated. "Oh."

"Next version incoming."

"Wait, wha—"

Ross reared back and punched him in the face again.

Max awoke to a Yankar full of werewolves, then to one with carnivorous rocks, then to a magnetic reversal of poles, then to a universe without commas, then to a world where Heisenberg's uncertainty principle made sense, then to one with sentient raindrops that screamed as they fell to grisly deaths, then to a desert version where giant worms ruled the planet, on and on and on. At around shift 62, Max tapped out for a breather. He sprawled out on the cave floor with his eyes clamped shut.

"Jeez and crackers, my head is killing me."

"Not surprised," Ross said and cracked his knuckles.

"Are you sure this isn't doing any brain damage?"

"Nah. Every shift is a new noggin, so each version only gets the one wallop. It ain't health food, but a random knock isn't going to hurt you. However, you do get the pleasure of feeling every single one of them."

"Ugh, I would give anything for an aspirin and a cup of coffee."

"Maybe the next world will have some." Ross rolled his shoulders and balled his mitts. "Ready?"

"No, no, please no." Max squirmed and rose to a seated position. "Let's take five. I need to get some air."

"Fine by me." Ross took the opportunity to spread-eagle and groom his crotch.

Max grimaced. "Thanks for that."

Ross paused to sneer at Max. "Forgive me, delicate little flower. Did I give you the impression that I care about your sensibilities?"

"Yup, must be dick o'clock. Right on time."

Ross ignored him and returned to his crotch.

Max climbed to his feet, stretched away some aches and pains, then shuffled over to the door vines. He pulled them aside, unveiling the afternoon sunlight. The glare forced an arm over his head to shield his eyes. He stepped out onto the ledge and gazed around the forest. The lower canopy hung overhead, giving him a bird's eye view of the ground.

He inhaled a breath of fresh air and lowered to the ledge, allowing his legs to dangle. After a bout of needed solace, he noticed a faint chanting off in the distance. It grew louder and louder until a small band of primitive Yarnwal hunters emerged from a thicket. They had killed a boar-like creature and were returning to camp. Max studied them from afar. He turned to the cave to consult Ross, only to discover that the feline had already settled beside him. Max flinched and nearly fell off the ledge. He flailed for balance and covered his heart.

"Sweet Sagan, warn me next time."

"I'm a cat. We don't do courteous."

"Obviously." Max sighed and refocused on the hunting party. "So what's this version? I see some Yarnwal, but they look crude and barbaric."

"Yup, nothing special about this one. They haven't even learned to use their cognitive abilities yet."

"So how did I get here?"

"Standard abduction with heavy probing."

Max sighed and shook his head.

"Your captor was planning to sell you to an exotic meat market, but crashed here after a malfunction. You managed to escape, but he was killed and eaten by the Yarnwals. Oh sweet irony. And get this, the Yarnwals actually worship the busted ship. They have it on display inside their village."

Max slacked his jaw and turned to Ross. "A ship. There's a spaceship on the planet. Can we fix it and get the hell out of here?"

Ross snorted. "Sure, if you weren't an idiot and I gave a shit."

"Awe c'mon, this could work. It's the best opportunity we've had so far. Who knows how many blackouts it's going to take to get us to a spacefaring Yankar? I would rather give this a go than endure another round of pummels."

Ross narrowed his eyes.

"Pleeeease?" Max clasped his hands and groveled like a child trying to stay up past his bedtime.

"Just so we're clear, you want to sneak into a Yarnwal camp, repair a ship that you don't know how to repair, fly a ship that you don't know how to fly, and all without being discovered and thusly eaten by a tribe of lizard bears."

Max thought for a moment, then nodded. "Yup."

Ross stared at Max like a preteen trying to make sense of a rotary phone, then grunted and smirked in a rare moment of respect. "Okay then."

* * *

Nifan's hologram image strolled around the cargo bay of Zoey and Perra's freighter. The lower section of her lengthy robe wrapped around a forearm, giving her the look and feel of a modern Roman stateswoman. She studied the interiors of wall lockers and moseyed through a maze of crates, as if physically present in the room.

Zoey and Perra traded puzzled glances.

"How is this possible?" Zoey said. "The only hologram projection we have is in the cockpit, and that's a standard relay. How are you doing this?"

Nifan smirked at the couple. "What does it matter? I'm safe. You're trapped."

Perra sighed.

"Fair enough," Zoey said, then lowered her guard. "So what's the play here?"

"First things first. You're going to disarm yourselves and submit to the guards outside."

Muted thumps echoed from the airlock door, startling the pair into a light flinch. Zoey lobbed a stink eye at Nifan before snatching

Perra's pistol and returning them both to the wall locker. She latched it shut with a harsh clank and returned her attention to the hologram.

"There." Zoey gestured at Nifan with open palms, then slapped her thighs. "Scan us if you like. We're clean through and through."

"I already have."

Zoey grimaced.

Perra maintained her disbelieving cockeye.

"Now, if you would be so kind, please open the airlock door and raise your arms."

Zoey sighed and moped over to the airlock. Perra raised her arms and backed against the wall. Zoey scowled at their hologram captor as she slapped the control panel. Her arms raised as the door slid open, allowing three beefy guards in sleek uniforms to enter the ship with weapons drawn. Their pale skin and beady eyes made them look like mole-rats in a marching band. Zoey eyed their guns and recognized them as streamlined versions of the composite weapons they used in missions. She knew right away that they were outgunned and outmatched.

"Good girl," Nifan said, then turned to the head guard. "Bring them to my quarters."

The guard nodded as Nifan's image crackled away. He turned to Zoey with a no-nonsense manner and flicked his pistol, motioning to exit the vessel. She took a reluctant step and dropped out of the ship. She hit the pristine platform of a docking bay and Perra followed suit. They paused to ogle a polished interior full of advanced machinery and hovering droids. A handful of service bots eyed them with curious stares. Zoey glanced back at the freighter, now held in place by a powerful mag-lock. A pair of titanium tethers secured it to the platform.

She frowned. "Well, that negates a hasty escape."

Perra studied a glowing ceiling littered with mag tracks and wireless tech. "This is the most sophisticated service bay I have ever seen. It's beyond advanced. This is art."

"It's also a prison, sweetie. Stop admiring the jail cell."

The hulking guards fell to the platform one by one. The head guard took point without saying a word and walked towards a port entrance along the far wall. Zoey and Perra followed behind with the other two guards bringing up the rear. Zoey stared straight ahead while Perra continued her slack-jawed study of everything around them. They slipped into a spacious tunnel with rounded corners. A continuous strip of blue light glowed overhead. Zoey glanced down to a glossy black floor and caught Perra doing the same through a crystal clear reflection.

The head guard came to a stop at a pair of large doors. He turned to face the Mulgawats, forcing them to stop with the full weight of his stature. The other two guards halted soon after and stiffened to a ready position. The head guard glanced at the double doors, allowing an iris scanner to do its thing. A ping of confirmation followed and the doors slid open, revealing the inside of a gleaming elevator. The guard turned to the ladies, glanced into the elevator, then back to the ladies, then back into the elevator, over and over until Zoey got the memo. She sneered at the brute, then grabbed Perra's arm and ushered her inside. The other two guards stood their ground as the head guard stepped into the lift, pushing Zoey and Perra to the opposite sides. He turned to face the doors as they slid closed.

An anxious silence infected the car as it raised through the ship. Zoey, ever the vigilant mercenary, eyed the plasma pistol in the guard's hand. His grip tightened, creating the snapping sounds of tightening leather. Zoey lifted her gaze to his, only to find a narrowed eye staring back at her. She puckered her lips and resumed a forward gaze. Perra, on the other hand, was perfectly content studying the icy blue strip illuminating the cabin.

The hum of ascent ended with a shrill ding. The doors slid open, revealing the opulent abode of a 70's porn mogul (or a reasonable facsimile). The guard stepped into the room and assumed his regular post against the adjacent wall. Zoey and Perra stood inside the elevator car with mouths agape, drinking in the unexpected image. A sea of fur pelts covered the floor. Elegant marble columns lined the walls with chic art pieces in between. Curvy couches encircled asymmetric tables. An eclectic medley of decor bedecked every surface, creating a groovy tapestry of excess.

Nifan emerged from a side nook with a martini in hand, her hologram image now flesh and satin. "Come inside, my lovelies." Paying them no mind, she floated over to a lime green couch and lowered onto the cushions. She crossed her legs and leaned off to the side, assuming the facade of an uncaring socialite.

Zoey took a cautious step forward, then another, using each one to gauge the current reality, like a dog discovering a new part of the house. She glanced over to the pale-faced guard, who glanced back with a cold severity.

"He won't bite," Nifan said as she sipped her martini. "He will, however, rip the spine from your body should I command it."

The guard replied with the slightest of smirks, sending a chill down said spine.

"Please come in. If I wanted you dead, you would have been dead a long time ago."

Zoey and Perra traded a restive glance, gathered their wits, and stepped inside the elegant abode. Nifan grinned as they approached, maintaining eye contact through delicate sips. She motioned across a glass coffee table, commanding them to sit. The ladies complied and lowered onto the plush cushions. The abrupt comfort caused Perra to gasp, despite the unfortunate circumstances. Zoey crossed her arms and leaned back against the rear cushion. She cocked her jaw and raised her brow, conveying *okay, crazy dame. You caught us, wowed us, and dragged us up to your shagadelic swank pad by means of a beefcake mole man. What's the deal?*

"I must say, for the universe's most feared courier, you were surprisingly easy to catch."

Zoey huffed. "You fired an anchor beam in Federation space. Cruising space, no less, and under stealth tech. You broke a hundred laws before you flipped the switch."

Nifan smiled and offered a slight nod. "A risk, but one I was willing to take."

"For what intent? More blackmail bitching?"

Nifan narrowed her gaze. "The last time we spoke, you disrespected me inside my own haunt. You then proceeded to murder my head of security, forcing me into the black. I think it unwise to disrespect me when your ship rests inside mine."

"Halim was a war criminal," Perra said. "He deserved what he got."

Nifan sneered at Perra. "Look at that, The Omen's pet has a voice."

Perra frowned and shrunk away.

Zoey leaned forward. "Yeah, I stared into that psycho's eyes and pulled the trigger. And I would do it again, and again, and again. It's a pity that he couldn't die a thousand more deaths, each slower and more painful than the last. I refuse to apologize to you or to anyone else for making the 'verse an infinitely better place by killing that lunatic."

Nifan erupted with a hearty chuckle, deflating an air of tension. "You think I want an apology?" She tossed back the final sip of her martini and rose to fetch another. Muffled giggles needled the room as she floated over to a wet bar on the far wall. She plucked a shaker from a silver tray, topped off her drink, and speared a few olives with a bone pick.

Zoey and Perra traded nervous glances.

"Let me make one thing abundantly clear," Nifan said as she sauntered back to the couch. "You could have tortured Halim for months on end for all I cared. He was an effective ruse, a shiny lure cast into the great black sea."

"Bait for Essien, we know." Zoey scooched forward and pointed at Nifan. "Which, I might add, you also used *us* for. You killed the bitch and destroyed the entire Varokin fleet. You got what you wanted, so what's the problem? You mad that you lost your Hollow Hold princess palace? Is that it? Can't say I much give a shit considering the hell you put us through."

Nifan glanced over to the guard and nodded. Without a trace of emotion, the brute started walking towards the table with a pistol in hand. Instinct drove Zoey and Perra to their feet, despite being powerless to react. Nifan grinned. Perra stepped back and scanned the room as Zoey hardened her stance and locked eyes with the wall of muscle. The beast tromped to a stop and loomed over the group. He stared at Zoey, then eyed the couch, then returned to Zoey, then back to the couch, over and over until Zoey lowered herself onto the cushions. Perra followed. The guard holstered his pistol, reached into a breast pocket, and pulled a battered comdev with a cracked screen. He tossed it to Zoey without warning, causing her to flinch-catch the device. She held it out in the palm of her hand like a live grenade.

"What's this?" she said, turning to Nifan.

"Power it on."

Zoey glanced at Perra, who reflected her reluctance. She took a measured breath, then tapped the surface. The device crackled with static and flickered to life. The start of a video clip filled the screen. She lifted a worried gaze to Nifan, who leaned back into the sofa and nodded.

"Go on, play it."

Zoey tapped the play icon. A fuzzy scene of a rocky area took shape, narrated by an alien tongue. The screen jerked and jostled as the device operator tramped towards a pillar of smoke in the distance. He approached what appeared to be the wreckage of a small spacecraft. A large figure came into view as he neared the scene. The brute was helping a smaller figure out of a mangled escape pod. The operator jogged towards the wreckage while grunting like a gorilla, unclear whether he wanted to help or scold the visitors for crashing onto his lawn. The large beast, clad in a pink tutu, turned to the camera and revealed himself as Jai Ferenhal. The image shifted focus to the unmistakable purple skull of Lord Essien. The operator gasped with sudden fright. Essien raised a plasma pistol and shot him. The blast rang through the tiny speakers, causing the device to rumble atop Zoey's hand. It fell from the operator's grip and landed face-up to the Hollow Hold sky, where battle debris from the Varokin fleet continued to rain into the atmosphere. Zoey swiped the video back and paused on the image of an irate Lord Essien. Perra covered her mouth.

"Any questions?" Nifan took another sip.

Zoey lowered the comdev onto the table and folded her hands in thought. After a bout of heavy contemplation, she returned her gaze to Nifan. "I assume this means that you want to finish the job."

Nifan grinned.

"And ... that you need us to play a part."

Nifan raised her drink for a solitary toast. "There's The Omen I know. Nice to have you back."

Zoey expelled a heavy sigh. She cupped her hands over her face and rubbed her forehead. Perra gripped her thigh while staring at the tarnished comdev. Nifan smirked at the sight and took another sip. The guard, still towering over the table like a misplaced statue, shifted his sunken eyes around the group without moving a single non-eyeball muscle.

Zoey dropped her hands and eyed Nifan with a solemn gaze. "Okay. What do you need us to do?"

CHAPTER 5

Lord Essien stood atop the throne platform inside the former Varokin headquarters. Jai and the other four Varokins stood around the platform with their plasma rifles cradled to their chests. The Dimathiens remained seated at their consoles, looking bored and deflated. One of them sighed. Another spun around in his swivel chair at a slow and pathetic pace. Essien loomed over the throne with a pistol in hand, tapping her thigh with waning patience. A splatter of green blood painted the back. Trevor's headless body slumped off to the side. The squishes of reassembling flesh broke the dead air. An eyehole reformed and sucked up the last drops of blood, causing Trevor to stir. He shook off the resulting headache, adjusted his posture, and lifted an annoyed gaze to Essien.

"You make an interesting argument," he said.

"All," Lord Essien said with a stern tone.

"Half."

"All."

"Three quarters."

"All."

"Most."

"All."

Trevor huffed. "I can't just relinquish full control of the Moreon fleet to your command. Do you know how long it took us to build it?"

"All."

Trevor groused. "Fine, I'll give you everything but two warships and a jump shuttle."

"All."

Trevor narrowed his eyes. "One warship and a promise to convert."

"You can have Jai as a conversion."

Jai furrowed his brow.

Trevor slapped the armrests and leapt to his feet. A lump on his face pulsed with anger as he shook a furious finger at Lord Essien. "I have already agreed to much more than you deserve. What the hell am I supposed to do with a groupie convert and one warsh—"

BLAM! Essien shot him in the face.

His headless body collapsed into the throne as blood and brain goo rained upon the platform. The groans of wearied Dimathiens filled the chamber.

* * *

Under the cover of night, Max and Ross snuck towards the Yarnwal camp. Ross took point, gliding over and around obstacles with Max trying to keep up. Every now and then, the tiger would stop and grumble as his human companion scrambled over roots and rocks. The glow of a large bonfire appeared in the distance, denoting the camp's location. Max stared at the dancing flame, which allowed his foot to catch a root tangle and send him flailing to the ground. He yelped before slamming face-first into the dirt.

Ross grimaced and glanced back at the clumsy human. His voice lowered to a harsh whisper. "You know, it's shit like that that will get us killed."

"Bite me, Hobbes," Max said, matching the whisper.

"That's racist."

plucking the twigs from his beard.

ave to cut me some slack."

evolution, you twit."

here. Stop being a dick."

ere too."

make that retort?"

shtick, remember?"

ng off his duds. "We're about to risk our

ultration, yet you still find the time to be an

We're only risking your life."

You know, my confidence in this mission

nose dive."

"Why, because I can't technically die?"

"That kind of skews your perspective, don't you think? What possible motivation do you have to see this through?"

"Are you kidding? This is going to be hilarious." Ross turned away and resumed his stealthy approach.

Max's frustration caused him to flail like a pouty toddler and yank his dreadlocks. The resulting pain conjured a yelp in his chest, but he swallowed it back and groaned instead. He slumped forward and followed the tiger.

Ross lurked around the perimeter of a wooden fence standing several meters tall. The wall surrounded the entire compound, an area about the size of a city block. The lower canopy hung overhead, concealing the Yarnwal camp from Yankar's towering beasts. It was safe and secluded space, in relative terms. Numerous bonfires reflected off the canopy leaves, giving the entire area a faint orange glow. Guards stood watch over the two main entrances, forcing Max and Ross into a climb. After a short hike, Ross came to a stop at a knobby log used in the wall. He peeked through a knothole and scanned the immediate area inside.

"Here's our entry point. Climb up and over this log. Meet me behind the mud hut to the right."

"Shouldn't we—"

Ross crouched for a split second and bounded to the top of the wall. With a claw and yank, he sailed over to the other side and landed with stealthy silence. Max watched through the knothole as Ross trotted over to a mud hut and settled behind it. He plopped into the dirt and started grooming a paw without a care in the world.

Max glanced up to the wall crest and took a deep breath. He jammed a toe into a knothole and started his non-feline ascent. His muscular frame made short work of the barrier, but an unexpected slip caused him to grunt and reset. Soon after, he raised a taut brow over the ridge like a special ops soldier emerging from a swamp. A collection of mud huts cluttered the ground beneath him, each with matching flags and adornments. A clan or family, perhaps. At the center of the village, bonfires raged with bands of Yarnwals dancing around them. Several donned leafy skirts and white paint, like an aboriginal tribe of lizard bears. Max glanced over to Ross behind the hut, who swung an open paw as if to say *anytime, dude*. Max rolled his eyes and tossed a leg over the top. With a final yank and dangle, he released his grip and landed on the other side. Not as graceful as a tiger, but the stomps and chants of the Yarnwals concealed his thump and stumble. Max regained his balance and jogged over to Ross.

"That was easier than I thought," Max said.

"What did you expect?"

"I dunno, something a bit more guarded and a little less scalable."

"The illusion of safety. Take human homes for instance. What sense does it make to put locks on doors, but then fill the exterior with panes of glass?"

Max paused for thought. "That's a good point. What the hell is wrong with us?"

"Nothing. Fear breeds irrationality and you are hardly unique in that regard. Not to point out the obvious, but the fear of losing your friends has you risking your life inside a camp full of hostile beasts."

"But that's love."

"The ultimate irrationality."

Max grimaced.

Ross peeked around the hut and studied the area. "You see the central bonfire?"

Max peered over his shoulder. "Yeah."

"The ship is off to the left. The tribe is in the middle of a worship ritual, so we can sneak off to the right and assess a reasonable approach. We'll find a good vantage point and proceed once they wrap up. Sound good?"

"Why are you asking me?"

"This is your show, knob head."

"Like I know what the hell I'm doing."

"That much is obvious."

"Just, ugh, fine. Yes, that sounds good."

"Was that so hard?"

Max glared at the feline.

"Follow me, wanker."

They sneaked around the perimeter, hiding behind huts and woodpiles. A rack of hanging meat reminded Max of his grumbling stomach. He paused to savor the aroma of a perfectly charred piece of, well, something. Ross paid him no mind, content to let him perish for lack of hunger control. After a moan and lip smack, Max snapped back to mission mode and hurried to catch up. Ross came to a stop behind a large log stack resting beside a storage hut. An overhang of dried leaves created the perfect hidden wedge. Ross took a seat as Max ducked inside. The stomps and chants of the Yarnwal ritual boomed nearby, allowing them to chat at a normal volume.

"Want to take a look?" Ross said, then resumed his paw grooming.

Max raised from a crouch and peered over the stack. A bustling crowd of Yarnwals strutted and stomped around a roaring bonfire. A select group danced around the center as ceremonial leaders, wearing white paint and ornate attire. They jumped and flailed as if possessed. Beaded necklaces bounced and swayed with every jerky movement.

Looming behind the crowd was a large black ship with a round hull. The lifeless vessel rested upon an elevated platform made of thick logs. Towering pylons stretched its tentacles to either side, creating the impression of a mounted octopus. Various flags and accoutrements hung from the tendrils. Every now and then, the raving mob threw their arms into the air and bowed to the machine, as if prepping for a virgin sacrifice. Ross paused his grooming session to address the gaping jaw and unblinking stare of his human companion.

"What's wrong?" he said.

"That's the ship?"

"Obviously. Why?"

Max slogged his gaze over to Ross and gestured to the spidery contraption. "That ... is a Ripper."

"So?"

"*So?* Are you not the slightest bit curious why a Varokin fighter ship is marooned on Yankar?"

"Red, blue, pink with tassels, the hell does it matter? It's a ship, ain't it?"

"Yeah, in the sense that a great white shark is a fish."

"So we'll have some firepower. Seems like a plus."

"Dude, that thing is more loaded than Lindsay Lohan on a weekend bender. The air conditioning and nuclear hellfire controls are on the same damn console. Turning on the radio could mean Death Starring a planet."

"You're overthinking this."

"Why are you so dismissive?"

"Why are you such a wuss?"

"Why are you such an asshole?"

"Why is a flock of crows called a murder?"

"Why—what?"

"Oh, sorry. I was bored of this conversation and decided to change it."

Max stammered in response.

"So you don't know? I'm genuinely curious. A gaggle of geese makes more sense than a murder of crows."

Max glared at the feline, then turned his attention to the flying death machine. He sighed, grunted, and thumped his forehead onto the log pile.

* * *

With a flick of the wrist, Nifan polished off her martini and stood from the couch. She wound the train of her dress around an arm and floated towards the wet bar behind Zoey and Perra. Nifan tossed them a casual glance as she passed, blinking her cobalt eyes with the callous indifference of an alcoholic mother. She reached the counter and plunked the martini glass on top. Ice cubes fell into a shaker, followed by a healthy pour of clear liquor and a dollop of green fluid that resembled battery acid. She shook the contents and poured herself another drink. The concoction started to glow, lifting a sly grin on her face. She nabbed the glass, turned towards the Mulgawats, and leaned back on the counter. Zoey and Perra stared back at her with cautious intrigue.

"What I want from you two is quite simple," Nifan said before taking a first sip. "I want you to make a delivery."

Zoey and Perra glanced at each other.

"Um, you could have just paid us for that service like a normal psycho," Zoey said.

Nifan chuckled. "I doubt you would have accepted."

"Illegal goods?" Perra said in a meek voice.

"I prefer to call them ... problematic."

Zoey scoffed. "Lemme guess, bioweapon? Dirty bomb? Some other clichéd spy shit?"

Nifan swirled her drink. "Cleaver nukes."

Perra gasped and covered her mouth.

"*What?*" Zoey leapt to her feet. She stepped around the couch towards Nifan, prompting the beefy guard to take a step of his own. Zoey slowed her pace in response. "Correct me if I'm wrong, and I hope to Tim that I am, but I think I just heard you say that you expect us to haul Loken-banned nuclear munitions. The very same munitions, I might add, that are notorious for their volatility."

"Not some," Nifan said. "50 crates are being loaded into your ship as we speak."

Zoey shuddered.

Perra started to tremble.

A tense silence infected the room.

"And if we refuse?" Zoey said in a subdued tone.

"Do you really have to ask that question?"

Zoey expelled a fluttering breath.

Nifan floated around a stunned Zoey on her way back to the couch. She set the glowing martini on the table, lowered to the cushion, and resumed her casual lean. A flick of her wrist sent the guard back to his station. "The PCDS has no jurisdiction, making it more powerful than most military outfits. The only limitation is *what* you carry, not where or how. It's the optimal way to smuggle some less than savory cargo."

"Less than savory?" Zoey said as she turned to Nifan. "That's a cute way to describe the peril you're saddling us with. A single unit is unstable enough, but 50 *crates*? That is a risk beyond comprehension. They would likely kill *us* long before delivery."

Nifan smirked. "Then I suggest you be careful."

Zoey clenched her jaw and bowed her head.

"I trust you understand the necessity of disclosure. You are not delivering bonbons to some fat cow in the reef."

"What's the destination?" Perra said.

"You will rendezvous with a merc named Migg at the Terramesh. He is stationed at a remote outpost on Grondon. Each crate carries its own cloak and beacon. Coordinates will be delivered once you are in the vicinity and contents have been verified. Do you understand?"

Perra turned to Zoey, who slowly nodded.

"Good girl."

Perra scrunched her brow. "Wait, what does this have to do with Lord Essien?"

"Jarovy is the Varokin stronghold."

"Well, it *was*. You destroyed their fleet, remember?"

Nifan shifted her posture. "Jarovy was usurped by the Moreons, a religious sect that spread throughout the mesh. Lord Essien is plotting to regroup with the aid of their fleet. Suffice to say, this cannot happen."

The realization hit Zoey like a punch the stomach. She crossed her arms and glared at Nifan. "You want to implode the mesh."

Nifan glared back and took another sip.

Zoey huffed. "That's a tad extreme for an assassination, don't you think?"

"I should also mention that each crate carries its own remote detonator. Should you wander off course or emit an unauthorized signal, I will chalk this up to an unfortunate accident." She swirled the glowing martini and took another sip, allowing the silence to fester. "If you do your job and do it well, you need not worry. Your reassurance is standing by the door."

Zoey eyed the guard, who stared back at her through an icy gaze. She turned to Nifan, then back to the guard, then back to Nifan. "You lost me."

"Henry is going with you."

Perra snorted. "*Henry*? I would have expected Crusher, or Zargoth."

Henry eyed Perra and narrowed his gaze by a tiny sliver, conjuring enough menace to quell her amusement.

"Henry is a valuable and trusted confidant. If he's safe, then you're safe. He will part ways at the rendezvous point and you are to remain there until he returns. Once he does, you will return him to me."

"What will he be doing?" Zoey said.

"What he is tasked to do."

"For how long?"

"As long as it takes."

Zoey started to respond, but sighed instead.

"Any more silly questions?"

"Just one."

Zoey gripped her hips and moseyed over to Henry. She stopped beneath his chin, close enough to smell his heated breath. Her lips shifted as she stared into his sunken eyes. Yellow orbs with pale irises stared back, unblinking and full of menace. Zoey chewed on her lip as she looked him over, studying the meat tower like a crafty nerd sizing up a bully. She turned to Nifan and pointed at Henry.

"What the hell is he? The guy looks like a shaved Shar-Pei in a pimp suit."

Henry ruffled his brow.

Nifan emitted a polite chuckle. "Henry is a Boobybork, a race—"

Zoey and Perra burst into laughter, filling the room with howls and wails. Perra gripped her chest and doubled over, slapping the table between gasps. Zoey covered her mouth with both hands as squinting eyes squeezed tears down her cheeks. Even Nifan joined the foolery, grinning between soft chuckles. Henry maintained his statuesque presence, despite the unfortunate goading.

"Henry the Boobybork," Zoey said through teary-eyed laughter, then punched his shoulder.

The collective mockery drew a grimace and head shake from the brute.

Nifan took a sip and regained her composure. "As I was saying, a race known for their resilience and long life spans. They come from a desolate planet with scarce resources and crushing gravity. As a result, they can adapt to and survive almost anywhere. They can even withstand the vacuum of space for hours on end. Their tenacity is unmatched in the biological realm."

"In other words, he's an ideal errand boy."

"I prefer to think of him as an unkillable enforcer."

"A delightful twist to this charade." Zoey moseyed back to the couch and plopped beside Perra. "So what's the gain then? Why sever the mesh to kill a mark?"

Nifan glanced away as if to wave off the question. She sighed and took another sip before returning her cobalt eyes to Zoey. "Just do your job."

CHAPTER 6

Trevor and Lord Essien were locked in a staring contest atop the throne platform. Essien loomed over him while tapping her thigh with the pistol. Trevor glared up from the throne with hands folded into the steeple of an overzealous comic book villain. He rapped his fingertips, trying to convey some weighted contemplation, but came across more like a campy cosplayer. The Dimathien minions continued to nurse their collective boredom under the watchful gazes of Jai and the Varokin goons.

"Two scooters, a hover cart, and all the coffee makers."

Essien chuckled and shook her head, as if trying to talk tech to a Luddite. "What part of *all* do you not understand?" She started to raise the pistol.

"Wait! Wait." Trevor sighed and slumped in the throne. "You have to give me something. Otherwise, the flock will not respect my authority."

"And controlling the coffee makers will inspire awe?"

Trevor gnawed at his cheek. "I can spin it."

"For that matter, why the coffee makers? I was under the impression that you could not partake."

"This is religion, not checkers. We seek to control the will and actions of others."

Essien leaned forward and gripped the armrests, putting them face to face. Her silvery eyes pierced him with a deep disdain. "And that is why you will never beat someone like me. I never seek control, only advantage."

Trevor puckered his lips and recoiled.

Essien smirked, then resumed her rigid posture. "Zwaq, eliminate all intruders."

"Wait, *what?* You had that ability all this ti—"

ZOT! Laser turrets emerged from the ceiling panels and blasted every Dimathien. Their bodies exploded, showering the room with blood and guts like bursting water balloons. The Varokin guards retained their poise as innards smacked them from all directions. Jai cringed under the gory deluge, then groaned at the sight of his gunked-up suit.

"Shut up, you big baby," Essien said as she sauntered off the platform. "They'll reassemble in a tick and your suit will be fine."

"Still gross." Jai grimaced as he flung some snotty mucus from his fingertips.

Essien floated by him on her way to the entrance doors. She paused to address a minion. "Tell that moron—"

"Moreon," Jai said.

"I didn't misspeak, fuckface." Essien glared at Jai, who sighed and bowed his head. "Tell that *moron* to meet me on the terrace. As much as it pains me to admit, I still need him and his merry band of fruitcakes."

The minion nodded.

Essien patted her thigh. "Jai, come."

Jai frowned and shuffled to her side.

Their footsteps squished through a fresh layer of carnage as they exited the room.

* * *

Max studied the Yarnwal dance troupe with wide-eyed fascination as Ross finished up a lengthy grooming session. With a final hoot and stomp, the ceremony came to a sharp conclusion. Chants faded into the dull roar of post-worship conversation. The crowd dispersed in all directions as tribe members headed home for the evening. Several tramped by the log stack, oblivious to the presence of the human and feline intruders. A handful of Yarnwals remained behind, content to chat around a dwindling bonfire. Max eyed them with annoyance, as their loafing thwarted a time-sensitive escape plan.

"Ugh, how are we going to get by them?"

Ross glanced up from a paw lick to study the lingering Yarnwals. A group of four prattled around a circle. One of them gripped a ceremonial spear as he wiped paint from his face with a tattered cloth. The other three seemed perfectly content to stand around in their scaly birthday suits. Their bulky frames kept Max at a safe distance, who griped and grumbled like a commuter stuck in traffic. Ross sighed and moseyed out from behind the log pile.

"Whoa, whoa, what the hell are you doing?" Max said with a harsh whisper.

Ross ignored him and maintained a casual stroll out into the ritual pit. Max gawked in horror as the cat approached the Yarnwals like a post-nap lion wandering the Serengeti. Ross halted behind the group, parked his bum, and cleared his throat. All four turned to the tiger and froze with fright. The crackle of bonfire embers broke a choking silence. Ross traded glances with each pair of widened eyes as tensions infected the air. The painted tribesman started to raise his spear, prompting the feline to lock eyes and growl. Rows of sharp teeth appeared behind giant fangs. The group started to back away at a slow and prudent pace. Ross matched each step, growling louder with each advance. The tiger erupted with a husky roar, causing the group to scream and scatter. The spear clanked to a rest beside the fire pit. Ross turned to Max as the entire camp began to stir.

"You coming or what?"

Max scampered out from behind the stack and sprinted towards Ross, who started trotting towards the Ripper ship. Yarnwals emerged from their huts with weapons in hand, alerted to the intrusion. The camp awoke with a bellow and converged on the central pit. Ross bounded up a crude set of stairs and onto the Ripper platform. Max followed him up, mumbling *shit shit shit* the entire way. The rounded vessel stood several meters tall with four tendrils protruding from either side. Ross smirked at his own reflection in the shiny black hull as he trotted towards the airlock in the rear. The yelps of furious warriors grew louder as the tribe neared the platform. A quick swipe and scan opened the airlock door, allowing Ross to enter. Max scurried around the vessel and dove inside before the door slid shut.

Soon after, a Yarnwal warrior slammed into the front of the ship and sprawled across the viewport like a meaty bug on a windshield. Max yelped and skittered backwards along the floor. Ross remained in a gargoyle stance, undeterred by the attack. Another warrior followed, then another, on and on until their cumulative mass covered the entire viewport. Their widened eyes radiated the unbridled rage of a father catching a boy bone-deep in his daughter. Max's gaze darted around the Ripper interior. He gasped and trembled, feeling an equivalent need to dive out of a window.

"Calm down," Ross said. "We're inside and they're not. At this very moment, you are the safest you have ever been on this planet."

Max covered his racing heart. "They can't get in?"

"It's a primitive tribe of lizard bears versus a high-tech death machine from outer space. It might as well be an army of guinea pigs attacking a monster truck. We're fine."

Max glanced around a sea of angry eyeballs. One of the warriors sneezed, splattering the viewport with mucus. The slimy wad crawled down to the next warrior, causing a mild ruckus. Another warrior started to lick the glass, for reasons known only to him. Max inhaled a deep breath to reset his nerves, then refocused on the task at hand. "Okay, so what now?"

"We fix the ship. Or rather, I tell you what to do and you fix the ship."

Max nodded, rubbed his wearied eyes, and plunked his head

against the wall. With danger averted and adrenaline tapped, fatigue started to infect his mind.

"Remember, this is all for naught if you fall asleep. So, chop-chop."

"Yeah, yeah, okay." Max nodded like a drunk fighting a blackout. "What do I need to do?"

Ross unsheathed a claw and hooked a wall panel. With a flick of the wrist, the panel clanked onto the floor, exposing a mess of tubes and wires.

Max groaned.

For the next several hours, Ross guided Max through a series of ship repairs. A splice here, a reroute there, a patch and hack to restore operations to the life support. Max took to the task like a duck to water, thrilled to apply everything he had learned as Perra's protégé. Before long, he started to finish Ross's sentences and jump to the next repair. A sense of worth and accomplishment filled his mind, offsetting a deep longing for his friends.

After the first hour, the Yarnwal warriors dropped their rage for a healthy dose of curiosity. A few even fetched some bricklebom (the local equivalent of popcorn). Max dangled his legs from inside a cramped cubby. The audience gasped with every conk and curse, as if watching a horror movie at an old drive-in theater.

Ross angled for a better view. "Okay, you see that green connector in the upper right corner?"

Max scanned the interior. "Um, yeah."

"Attach the feeder hose—"

"—and lock the uplink. On it." Max fed the hose through a mess of wires and twisted it into the port. A tap and flick reset the uplink. "Done."

"And with that, this squid should be space worthy."

"Hell yeah!" Max celebrated with a grunt and fist-pump, but bonked his head against the interior frame. The resulting curses triggered another round of gasps and mumbles from the audience. He snaked his way out of the cubby, climbed to his feet, and indulged in a much-needed backstretch. "So what exactly did we just do?"

"We repaired an ionic conduit and rerouted some flark switch-es."

Max nodded and actually understood.

"The big problem was the reclaimers. They were busted up be-yond repair, hence the emergency landing. So, we just bypassed them and fed the tanks directly into the ventilation system. In other words, you'll be breathing pure oxygen."

Max scrunched his brow. "Wait, isn't that toxic?"

"Only for extended periods of time. You'll be fine for a few hours, enough to get you into orbit and knock your ass out." Ross pantomimed an uppercut.

Max deflated a bit. "Yeah, but ... won't this version of me get poisoned and die?"

"Probably."

"I, um ... hmm."

"This was your plan, genius. Don't tell me you're having second thoughts."

Max frowned like an innocent nipper having uncovered the Santa Clause lie.

Ross sighed. "Tell you what, after you shift away, I will wake your alter ego and give him the lowdown. He should have a 10-hour buffer before brain damage, which gives us plenty of time to iron out the weirdness. Sound good?"

"What if he doesn't want to return?"

"Then I imagine he'll die."

"Can you not jump somewhere else?"

"In a rogue Ripper? That won't raise any eyebrows."

Max whimpered.

"This is hardly the time for an existential crisis. Infinite univers-es, infinite possibilities."

"I know, but—"

"But nothing. At this very moment, there are countless versions of you getting eaten by the Yarnwals because you never made it to the ship. And trust me, those are the lucky ones. In a couple versions, the Yarnwals prefer to tenderize their meals in very unsettling ways.

Don't think about it, just look out for you."

Max bowed his head and began to tear. He glanced at the viewport where numerous Yarnwals stared back at him through watering eyes. They had no idea what was going on, but dammit, they knew an emotional scene when they saw one.

Ross sauntered up to the pilot seat and hovered a paw over the console. Eager faces watched his every move. A few recoiled, unsure of what would happen next, but remained hooked on the unfolding drama.

Ross turned to Max. "Just say the word."

Max sniffled, wiped his eyes, and nodded. "You're right. Let's blow this popsicle stand."

"Word to the wise, don't use that expression away from Earth. It has an entirely different connotation that I doubt you're prepared to deal with."

Max cringed. "Noted."

Ross thumped the console.

Chirps and pings filled the cockpit as the control panel sputtered to life. Whirs and hums joined the party as the nav computer came online. Icons blinked and switches glowed. Coms crackled and the beacon rang. The entire ship rumbled as systems reconfigured and stabilized. The Ripper stirred as it woke from a long hibernation.

The Yarnwal audience yelped and scurried away from the viewport, save for one captivated youngster. Her father rushed back and snatched her from the glass as a trail of red lights climbed down the tentacles. The giant metal octopus exhaled a breath of resurrection.

Max and Ross traded a well-deserved high five.

Then the ground shook.

Max stumbled into a wall. "Was that us?"

"Not sure." Ross glanced around the cabin.

"Maybe a burst disc?"

"Possibly."

The ground shook again.

They locked eyes.

"Definitely not us," Ross said with a twinge of worry.

Max leaned towards the viewport and gazed out across the village. Not a Yarnwal in sight. "Um, I don't see anyone. Did they all leave the—"

Another shake, this time much closer.

The hull whined upon the platform.

Max and Ross pressed their faces to the viewport, then lifted widened eyes to the treetops.

A massive tree trunk split the canopy and slammed into the ground just outside of the village, rumbling the area on impact. Dirt and dust spilled off the village huts. A cloud of embers belched from the fire pit. Log piles and meat racks collapsed. Max and Ross gawked at the towering tree that fell from the heavens. Upon further scrutiny, they noticed a veneer of scaly bark and giant clawed roots. Not so much a tree as the colossal shin of a Yankar monster. The canopy cracked and rustled, showering branches onto the ground. Moments later, the gigantic head of a reptilian beast poked through the foliage. Nostrils the size of kiddy pools expelled puffs of heated breath. A pair of glowing red eyes scanned the village before fixating on the Ripper.

Ross gulped. "I should probably mention that creatures here are attracted to electrical signals. Very important. Fun fact for everyone."

Max slogged a horrified gaze over to the tiger. "So what you're saying, purely and simply, is that we just summoned Godzilla."

"Yeah, pretty much."

The creature roared with the ferocity of a million air raid sirens. Bands of saliva detached from meter-long fangs and splashed into the dirt. A dollop hit the fire pit and snuffed it out in a large puff of steam, as if dousing it with a bathtub. The monster loomed over the Ripper and chomped down on the hull, yanking Max and Ross off their feet. The interior creaked and whined as the beast adjusted its bite. Instinct drove Max into the pilot seat. Hurried hands strapped in as the ship raised into the air. Ross pinned himself to a corner, digging claws into the walls and floor. The metal tentacles hung to either side of the creature's jaws like a steampunk mustache. Max grabbed the yoke while staring down the gullet of the beast.

"What the hell do I do?!"

"Red squares on the right of the—" The ship jerked and jostled. "—fuel line bar! Tap them all to green!"

Max complied. "Now what?!"

"Switches overhead! Flick the entire second row!"

Max flicked them all. "Done!"

"Big green icon on the right side! Hit it!"

Max thumped the icon with a hard fist.

Thrusters ignited, which merely angered the beast. Blue flames turned gooey saliva into puffs of steam. Another roar sprayed the viewport with throat mucus. The beast whipped its head from side to side, trying to extinguish the nuisance. An enormous tongue wrapped around the hull and pulled the ship deeper into its throat.

Max yelped with every plunge.

Ross gnashed his teeth and adjusted his grip. "Okay, this one's gonna be tricky. You ready?"

"No, give me a minute to think about it."

"Um, well—"

"Of course I'm ready! Give me the goddamn orders!"

Ross sneered in response.

The ship jostled with another gulp.

"Do you see the eight blue indicators on the left?"

"Yeah."

"Hit the big red icon beneath 'em."

"Got it."

"Now tap 'em all on."

"Done."

A crimson glow filled the monster's throat as the Ripper tendrils armed for battle.

"When I say go, you need to swipe the second ladder up to full power, hit the lower icon again, then whip the yoke hard left. Understand?"

"Got it."

"Ready?"

"Ready."

Max hovered a shaking palm over the console, waiting for the signal. Ross narrowed his eyes and held his breath. The creature gulped again, bringing the vessel down into the throat.

"Now!"

Max swiped the ladder.

The tendrils stirred.

Max slapped the icon.

The tendrils shot out the creature's neck, spraying blood over the village and drawing a screech.

Max yanked the yoke hard left.

The ship spun and sliced through the wall of flesh.

The Ripper decapitated the beast.

An enormous head spun through the air and slammed into the earth. The headless body leaned off to the side and crashed through the canopy, hooking vines and snapping branches on its way down. The tower of flesh crashed onto the ground, lifting a tidal wave of dust and dirt. The impact climbed into the trees, rustling the leaves and creaking trunks. Blood gushed from head and neck stump, forming crimson lakes around the body.

Max and Ross felt the impact from inside the hovering Ripper. Ross retracted his claws, rose from the corner, and rolled his shoulders. Max maintained his death-grip on the control yoke. Saucer-like eyes stared into a viewport caked in blood and guts. Ross strolled up beside him, studied the carnage, then tapped a console icon. A stream of water hit the glass as a pair of wipers swiped it clean. Max inhaled a deep breath, held it for a tick, then exhaled a long fluttering sigh. Ross grinned and bumped his shoulder.

"Nicely done."

Max closed his eyes, steadied his nerves, then screamed at the top of his lungs.

Ross flinched into a stumble. "Jeebus."

Max released his grip and melted into the seat. "Sorry. Had some pent-up horror there."

"You do realize what just happened, right?"

Max slogged his gaze over to Ross.

"You, brave samurai, have bested the mighty Gozira!" Ross clasped his paws and bowed.

"That's racist ... and chronologically inaccurate."

A muted roar hooked their attention. It seemed to come from all directions, like a blanket of static washing over the vessel. Max glanced around the cabin.

"What the hell is that?"

Ross grinned. "Cheering."

"The Yarnwals are cheering? But, we nearly destroyed their village."

"No, you just filled their pantry. They'll be gnawing on Godzilla jerky for the next 20 winters."

A slight grin lifted Max's cheek.

"You did a good thing, Earthman."

"Thanks, buddy."

"On that note, let's orally pleasure a row of hairy naked men on a cold park bench."

"Wha—*what?*"

"Oh, sorry. I meant, let's blow this popsicle stand."

"That's ... wow."

"Semantics, dude."

Max swiped an icon ladder to full capacity, igniting the main engine. He gripped the yoke and pulled back, angling the ship to a maze of branches. Ross smirked at his longtime companion like a proud father.

"You got this?"

"Easy peasy lemon squeezy."

"Um, you might not want to—"

"Shut up. I don't want to know."

Max grabbed the throttle and thrust forward. The Ripper surged upwards on a pillar of flame. It darted through the Yankar treetops and burst through the upper canopy. The spidery ship sliced through the atmosphere, leaving a fiery trail in its wake. The rumble softened to a hum as the vessel entered the blackness of open space. A twinkling sea filled the viewport, drawing a wide smile on Max's face.

Ross tapped his shoulder. "Oh, and one more thing."

Max turned to Ross, who reared back and punched him in the face.

CHAPTER 7

Zoey and Perra stood outside of their tiny freighter under the watchful eye of Henry. Perra resumed her giddy study of the advanced service bay while Zoey and Henry traded spiteful glances.

Another minion wheeled a final crate of cleaver nukes to the ship. He took extra care to hoist the black box and place it just inside the airlock. A yellow logo adorned each crate, the emblem of a toy company known for bobblehead dolls. Zoey shook her head as the minion climbed inside the ship and stacked the crate upon the others, completing a perfect rectangle of horror. Another pair of minions climbed inside and started the delicate process of latching the crates down without blowing up the entire stealth vessel. After a double-check, triple-check, and quadruple-check, the minions exited the ship and resumed their normal tasks in the service bay. The head minion paused to salute Henry, who responded with a slight nod.

Henry turned to Zoey, then to the airlock, then back to Zoey, then back to the airlock, then back—

"Yes, yes, I get it," Zoey said, adding an eye roll.

She nudged Perra and they both climbed into the ship.

Henry followed them inside and the door slid shut. He glanced around the cargo bay and decided to stand against the wall adjacent to the airlock. After all, he was a guard and something was going to get guarded, dammit.

Soon after, the hologram image of Nifan materialized in the bay, still cloaked in her silky ensemble. She studied the crate stacks, then turned to Henry. "All set?"

Henry nodded.

"Good." She turned to Zoey and Perra standing by the cockpit corridor. "As for you ladies, I trust you will handle this particular cargo with the utmost caution."

"As if you needed to tell us," Perra said.

"Not to point out the obvious, my dear, but The Omen is known for her shrewd yet reckless demeanor. This is hardly the time to indulge a headstrong nature."

Zoey narrowed her eyes in response.

Nifan moseyed beside the tidy crate stack. She eyed the belt latches and slid a palm down the side, causing Perra to slack her jaw.

"You can feel them?"

"Yes," Nifan said in a dismissive tone.

"Holographic sensory?" She turned a stupefied gaze to Zoey. "I didn't know that tech even existed."

Nifan rubbed a mote of dust between her fingertips. She flicked it away and glanced at Perra. "Now you do."

"How does that even work? I mean—"

Zoey snatched Perra's wrist.

Nifan wandered over to the pair, bringing them face to face. "To recap, Migg will contact you once you are in range of Grondon. Do as he says and mind your lip. He is not one to trifle with."

Zoey sighed, then nodded.

"Good girl." She grinned and turned to Henry. "Contact me immediately once—" Nifan caught herself and glanced at Zoey. "Once the crow is in the basket."

Henry nodded.

Zoey and Perra traded worried glances.

"I leave you with a quote from a cunning vixen." Nifan steeled her gaze. "Good luck, and don't fuck it up."

The hologram crackled away.

Zoey exhaled a weighted breath and stepped over to the stack of horrors. She inspected the latches, making sure that each belt was secured to the floor. Perra joined her with lips taut and arms crossed. She eyed one of the whimsy yellow logos and sighed.

"If only they were bobbleheads."

"What do you think are the chances we make it there in one piece?"

"Do you want an honest or optimistic opinion?"

"Are either of them good?"

"Not really."

"Then let's go with optimist."

"Well, at least we won't feel anything. I can take a little solace in that." She brushed Zoey's waist and wandered up to the cockpit.

Zoey eyed Henry over by the airlock. "Does it not bother you that we're all trapped inside a tiny ship full of unstable nuclear weapons?"

Henry blinked.

"Your conversational acumen is exhilarating."

Zoey hiked towards the cockpit, careful to stay light on her feet. Perra sat in the co-pilot chair with hands folded in her lap. Zoey slipped through the corridor and plopped into her seat. She reached for a drive icon, but the console was dark and lifeless.

"Still disabled," Perra said.

"Great. So what now?"

"I guess we wait."

Soon after, Henry squeezed through the narrow tunnel and popped into the cockpit. He twisted around the cramp confines, knocking the backs of chairs like an unruly kid on an airplane. Zoey and Perra grimaced with every jostle. He unlatched the wall seat behind Perra and lowered his beefy body onto a cushion many sizes too small. A fumble for belts and buckles drew pitiful smirks from the ladies. With a final yank and click, Henry latched in for safety. Or rather, the illusion of safety considering the payload. He adjusted his posture, cracked his neck, and met eyes with a bewildered Zoey. She studied the peculiar image, like a hippo perched upon a stepstool. At that moment, the following unspoken conversation transpired.

Do you know how dumb you look?

I can kill you with my pinkie.

Still, you look ridiculous.

I can kill you with the mere thought of killing you with my pinkie.

You look like a He-Man figure in a dollhouse.

I can kill you with—

I get it, jeez. Shut up, you wrinkly goblin.

A red haze crawled across the viewport, hooking their attention. Minions unlatched the titanium tethers, allowing the ship to float free. A pair of large docking doors opened to the blackness of space, its deadly vacuum held behind a transparent energy barrier. The red cocoon floated through with the freighter inside, pushed along by an anchor beam. A slight jostle caused the crates to rattle, forcing Zoey and Perra into tight cringes. Henry stared out into the big empty with zero concern, content to meet his end at any time. The beam detached and a wash of red static crackled across the viewport.

The console pinged to life, surrendering control back to the Mulgawats. Perra checked the system status and spun the main engines. Zoey flamed the thrusters and turned to face the stealth ship, which had already disappeared. She leaned forward and scanned the black abyss, like a curious child searching for her favorite constellation.

"That was something special," she said. "I mean, yeah, she kidnapped us and all, but I have never seen a ship with that much badassery. I can only imagine how much that set her back."

Perra snorted. "Nifan? I'd be shocked if she paid at all."

"Mhmm. She's been known to shake down the—" Zoey caught herself and eyed Perra.

They turned to Henry, who replied with a blank stare.

"Jeez, dude. I already forgot you were there."

"That's a wicked superpower," Perra said. "You're just one big info sponge, aren't you?"

Henry blinked.

Zoey and Perra met eyes and mentally agreed to temper their conversations for the foreseeable future. An awkward silence infected the cockpit as Perra entered the rendezvous coordinates into the nav system. A hologram rendition of the Terramesh appeared above the console. Spheres of all sizes connected to each other via a tangled web of steel.

"Tim almighty," Perra said. "Take a look at that jumbled mess."

"Grondon is in the center next to Jarovy."

Zoey reached inside the hologram and tapped one of the orbs. The display pinged and zoomed to the planet. An info panel of local races and dialects scrolled beside the rotating image. Perra studied the output for a moment, then ruffled her brow and slogged her gaze over to Zoey.

"How do you know that?"

"Know what?"

"The location of Grondon."

Zoey bit her lip and glanced at her lover. "I, um ... used to date a Grondo Bromwich."

"*What?* You never told me that."

"You never asked."

"Why would I even think to ask that question?"

"It was well before you, dear. It doesn't matter. Forget I said anything."

"Forget that you dated a Bromwich?" Perra cringed and shivered. "They're just so ... ugh."

"Speaking of the grotesque, I don't recall saying a damn thing about you dating that Kuiper weirdo."

"Like that's even the same thing."

"Well, they *are* known for their shiftiness and sexually aggressive—" Zoey caught herself again.

They turned to Henry, who had lifted an eyebrow.

Perra sighed and slumped into her seat. She crossed her arms and gestured at the viewport. "Let's just go."

Zoey tossed her a dirty look and swiped the console with healthy dose of melodrama. She initiated the jump drive and entered the

Terramesh coordinates. The power gauge filled to a solid bar and pinged. "You ready?"

Perra shrugged. "Whatever."

Zoey sighed and thumped the jump icon.

A streak of purple light ripped through the black sea and swallowed the ship.

* * *

Lord Essien gripped the terrace railing, overlooking the perpetual Jarovy cityscape from atop the Varokin tower. A longing smile lifted her cheeks as she watched shuttles and cutters slice through a thick haze of pollution. The tarnished facades of towers rose from the planet surface, resembling rusty knives pointing up to the heavens. Massive planetary bodies loomed in the sky, replacing the blackness of space with the rustic hues of earth and metal. Tangles of twisted steel bound each planet to the Jarovy surface, as if yanked together by a godlike Spider-Man. Twinkling bands of green light crisscrossed the surfaces, pulsing and glowing as giant conduits of perpetual commerce. Gazing up from the surface of Jarovy, one caught the impression of being trapped inside a cluster of grimy grapes.

But that's how Lord Essien liked it.

Jarovy was home. Or rather, the base of operations to one of the most ruthless criminal empires the universe had ever seen. The mighty Varokins ruled the underworld with an iron fist and quashed any that dared to challenge them. They reigned unopposed for a hundred years, serving as the rightful center of a boundless underbelly. Should the actions of a criminal cohort make universal news, one could damn well guarantee that the Varokins played a part. Put simply, only a fool doth fuck with the devil.

Lord Essien was that devil. That is, until she flushed the Varokin Empire down the proverbial toilet. She had made a tiny miscalculation that snuffed out her entire legacy. In an effort to dispatch her nemesis, she had brought umbrage to the table. A rookie mistake when facing the disarming calm of The Dossier. To put it another way, ninjas do not yodel as they sprint into battle.

Essien and Nifan were opposing forces that differed in almost every way. Essien employed brute force while Nifan wielded subtle influence. Essien dressed like an intergalactic thug while Nifan preferred the posh and tasteful attire of a ballroom belle. Essien liked *Star Wars* and Nifan liked *Star Trek*. Needless to say, the resentment ran deep. And as with most imposing adversaries, only one could survive.

For the first time in a long and murderous relationship, Nifan had a distinct advantage. With the Varokins depleted, Essien knew that Nifan would strike hard and fast, hence the burning need to restore some firepower. She had managed to recruit Trevor and the Moreons, so it was time to prep for the ensuing battle.

Jai stood behind her on the terrace, his posture stiff and attentive with hands locked behind his back, like a sergeant awaiting command. An odd sight considering his affinity for leisure suits. But Jai, ever the opportunist, decided to break the lingering silence. He cleared his throat, as if to prep Lord Essien for a dose of unwanted prattle. "Will you need me to command one of the Moreon ships, m'lord?"

"What I need you to command is your upper lip."

"I—yes, Lord Essien."

"And yet you continue to *not* command that lip."

Jai opened his mouth to apologize, but expelled a muted grunt instead.

Lord Essien turned to face him. She leaned back against the rail and crossed her arms, cloaked by the ceaseless traffic of Jarovy. Her eyes narrowed, as if to study a painting that made no goddamn sense. "It's like you go out of your way to ignore even the tiniest slivers of decorum."

Jai clamped his mouth shut.

Essien sighed. "But to answer your question, yes. I will need you to command one of the vessels. It seems you have been promoted."

"Thank you, Lord Essien. I consider it an honor to—"

She surged off the railing and got into his face, causing him to recoil like an abused dog. "Make no mistake about it, fuckface. You are in command by math, not merit." Essien grabbed his lapels and yanked him down to eye level. "You are not a Varokin, Jai. You will never be a Varokin. You are here at my behest, nothing more. Understand?"

"Y—"

She slapped him across the face. "Nod."

Jai nodded.

"Good boy," she said, then shoved him backwards.

Jai stumbled to a stop and glanced away.

Essien shook her head and returned to the railing. She expelled a heavy sigh and resumed her scan of the planet city. Her black fingernails rapped upon the metal, adding sharp tinks to the background rumble. She lowered to her forearms and glanced down the sides of the Varokin tower. A random collection of boxy vessels floated alongside. No rhyme, reason, or discernible cohesion, just a random mess of mangled hulls. Her precious fleet of Rippers, replaced by hovering trash cans. She bowed her head in disgust, like a Formula One racer forced behind the wheel of a Ford Pinto.

Trevor shuffled out of the main entrance and glided by the black shuttle resting on the landing pad. The short train of his white robe dragged behind, sweeping a path through the grimy platform. He waddled forward with arms folded across his belly and fabric draping from his wrists. His mask and hood were lowered, opting to meet the Jarovy pollution head-on. Just before reaching the terrace railing, he doubled over into a coughing fit. Trevor hacked and wheezed like a house cat working up a hairball. Lord Essien rolled her eyes, refusing to glance back or even acknowledge his presence. When the episode passed, he returned to his feet and carried on as if nothing had happened. He stepped to Essien's side and gazed out across the tarnished city. They stared straight ahead, like a pair of tourists drinking in the skyline.

Trevor grunt-coughed. "Breathing here is like sucking on a smog nozzle."

"You can suck on Jai's nozzle if you prefer."

Trevor glared at Essien. "You're not a nice lady."

Essien snorted and shook her head. "Tim almighty, it's like I'm partnering with a toddler."

"Apologies for the strong language, but it needed to be said." Trevor stiffened his chin and straightened his robe, assuming his moral high ground.

Essien refused to respond. She studied the Moreon fleet below them while running some mental math. "This is cute and all, but I'm not counting enough to mount a reasonable offensive. Hell, this is barely enough to secure the tower."

"Do not let your eyes fool you, madam. Every vessel you see carries an array of advanced plasma weaponry, not to mention ionic cannons and laser turrets."

"So you retrofitted dumpsters with battle tech."

Trevor shrugged. "Better to have a lot of good ships than a few great ships."

"But you don't even have *good* ships."

"We'll just have to agree to disagree."

Essien facepalmed herself.

"No need for concern. I am confident that the Moreon fleet will prove more than capable."

"Sweet fucking cheese farts, you haven't even tested—" She groaned in frustration, then lifted from the railing and gripped her waist. "Doesn't matter. Even with bomblets and nukes, you are still half a fleet short. Where are your shuttles and cruisers?"

Trevor glanced up to the sky, then returned a confused stare. "Do you not see them?"

Essien squinted as she studied a collection of freighters, cutters, and barges clustered high above the city. "Are you being cute about stealth tech or something? If so, you have earned another shot to the face."

Trevor stammered. "No, um, those." He pointed at the giant barges. "The big ones."

Essien examined the barges again, then closed her eyes and clenched her lips. "Are you trying to tell me that you *weaponized* trash barges?"

"Well, yeah. Pretty clever if you think about it. They are super strong, easy to fly, and have a bunch of nifty cubbies to hide fighters in."

"Barges are not battlecruisers, you lumpy dolt!"

"Why not? They're just as big and nearly as strong. They are cheap to fly, cheap to fix, and even cheaper to service. Plus, nobody suspects them. They are an ideal compromise if you ask me."

"I'm *not* asking you! I'm telling you that your fleet is a fucking farce!" She turned to Jai. "Will you talk some sense into this moron?"

"Moreon."

Essien gritted her teeth and balled her fists.

He raised his palms and took a step back, as if to say *hear me out, then hit me.*

"Don't you dare tell me that you agree with him."

"Just to play devil's advocate, consider your target. The Dossier expects a polished presence, a worthy foe mentally, tactically, *and* visually. This might give you an element of surprise that you never had before."

A tense silence fell upon the group.

Trevor gulped and took a step back.

Lord Essien grimaced as she hate-swallowed a bitter pill of truth. She gazed up into the polluted sky where a fleet of barges floated in the lower atmosphere. With lips taut and eyes narrowed, she dropped her gaze to the platform and barked in frustration.

Trevor chuckled. "I knew you would see it my way. You see, the Moreons have—"

Essien unlatched her plasma pistol and stomped over to Trevor, who stiffened with fright. Her furious gaze dug into his knotted brow, causing him to yelp. He turned to flee, but Essien grabbed him by a skull ridge and started blasting him in the neck.

BLAM! BLAM! BLAM! BLAM! BLAM!

Blood and guts showered the platform. Trevor's flailing body detached from his head and collapsed into a limp pile of flesh. The neck stump oozed green fluid over the terrace ledge. Lord Essien latched her pistol and gripped the head with both hands. Trevor's twitching eyes locked onto hers in his final moments of consciousness.

"The barges will do." She smiled, then drop-kicked the head over the railing.

CHAPTER 8

Max awoke as a bow-legged cowboy with a tiger, then as a skinless mountain gorilla with a tiger, then as a collection of sentient nanobots bound together as a human (with a tiger), then as a tiger with a human, which was weird.

But then it finally happened.

Max awoke slumped over the pilot seat in the standard punch-out position. A sleepy grunt and eye rub helped to gather his wayward wits. He straightened his posture and glanced around the Ripper cockpit. There, perched upon the console, was Ross as a tubby orange house cat. Max grinned at the sight, but Ross stared back at him in complete silence. Max chewed on his lip, then spread his arms in confusion.

"Well? Got anything to say?"

Ross smirked and shook his head. "Nope. Just going to enjoy the reveal."

Max scrunched his brow, then lowered his gaze to his chest. Or, more accurately, *her* chest. A pair of flesh pillows pushed out from beneath a set of leather duds. She gasped, then immediately groped herself. The soft breasts filled her hands perfectly (a relative assessment for any teenage boy). Max lifted, squeezed, lifted some more, squeezed again, and capped it all off with stiff-armed cleavage enhancer. She met eyes with Ross and grinned.

"I am totally okay with this."

"Oh, are you totally cool with boobs on demand? Pardon me whilst I fetch my shocked face."

"Bite me, Garfield."

"That's racist. And sexist now, I think."

Max slapped the armrests with a newfound gusto and leapt to her feet to commence a vigorous self-examination. The next order of business was, of course, a crotch grab. She cupped her nethers atop her knickers, then chuckled like a doofus.

"That's just ... weird. But hey, at least nothing will stick to my thighs anymore."

Further examination uncovered long brown hair pulled into a tight ponytail. A medium athletic frame filled a full set of leather garments, all dark purple with black accents. The garb was rugged for regular use, but restrained enough to look stylish while out and about. Max caught a glimpse of her reflection in the viewport and twisted her face from side to side. She retained features similar to her male self, much like a fraternal twin.

"So I take it that genders are flipped in this universe?"

"For humans, yes. The mechanism for sex determination is reversed here. You're a chick, your mother is your father, and all your girlfriends are boyfriends."

Max thought for a moment. "But I still like boobs."

"Of course you do. You always retain your psyche after shifting. But, that doesn't mean this body hasn't enjoyed its share of meat swords."

Max cringed.

"Not that it matters. Until you shift again, your status as a hetero male has converted you into a lesbian."

"Oh." Max puckered her lips and allowed her mind to wander. "What's my name here?"

"Max."

"No, I mean—"

"I know what you meant, minger. Your parents named you Maxine. Everyone still calls you Max."

"Huh, well that's convenient."

"No, just parallel."

"I, uh—" Max pinched her eyes closed for a brain reset. "Okay, so I'm a woman in tight leather who pilots a Ripper. What's the backstory here?"

Ross grinned. "I thought you'd never ask."

Max rolled her eyes and plopped back into the pilot seat. "Great, this should be fun." She took a measured breath and swayed an open palm, cueing Ross to proceed.

Ross stiffened his posture and puffed his chest, as if to prep for an impromptu briefing. His pursed face and lidded eyes conveyed a secret so juicy that it yearned to break free of its brainy prison. Ross snickered with untold delight, then released the beast. "You're a *me* worshipper."

Max raised an eyebrow. "Come again?"

"You, Maxine of Earth, are a Ferretian Crusader."

Max lowered the eyebrow.

"Remember that drunken reveal of mine that spawned a ferret-based Earth religion? Yeah, you're a devout follower. And the best part is, you're worshiping *me* and don't even know it."

Max huffed and glanced away.

Ross could barely contain his giddiness, cycling through snickers and clamped lips as if post-witness to a loud fart at a funeral.

Max crossed her arms and glared at the feline. "Okay, so I worship a giant purple banjo-playing ferret. How—"

Ross burst into laughter, forcing a wider stance to retain his perch. The console chirped with misplaced paw errors. Max sneered as the feline gasped and wheezed his way back to a reasonable composure.

"And how does this help our current predicament?"

"Brilliantly, to be honest. You're one of many Ferretian Crusaders who have been summoned to the Terramesh by Orantha Nifan to battle the Moreons. They—"

"Wait, did you just say *morons?*"

"Moreons. They're a religious sect that seized control of the Varokin Empire."

"So what you're telling me is that I'm a religious nut off to battle other religious nuts?"

Ross nodded. "Pretty much, yeah."

Max glanced away to mumble some choice curses, then regrouped with a heavy sigh. "And what is this place again, the Terramesh?"

"It's a bound cluster of 86 stolen planets."

Max opened her mouth to request clarification, but her brain responded with complete and total assurance that she neither wanted nor needed any further backstory. Her reply manifested as a twitching eyelid.

"The Moreons have partnered with Lord Essien in order to retain control of the Terramesh and shore up an armada. They plan to wage an all-out war with Nifan. Needless to say, The Dossier was none too pleased."

"Lord Essien is alive?"

"Yup. She and Jai Ferenhal survived the Hollow Hold assault."

"And now she leads ... the *Moreons?*"

Ross paused for thought. "Now that you say it out loud, it does seem rather silly."

"You think?"

"All the same, Zoey and Perra are in route to deliver a payload of cleaver nukes to a bloke named Migg, a Ferretian commander. Nifan plans to destroy the Terramesh in order to wipe out Lord Essien once and for all."

Max shook her head with a slow and steady pace that conveyed *holy shitballs, what have I gotten myself into?*

"And so, that's the plan. You'll fly this bird to the mesh and sneak back onto Zoey and Perra's freighter. Game, set, match. Bingo. Yahtzee. Borgal Dorgal."

Max leaned forward and dropped elbows to knees. She rubbed her face while her gray matter struggled to process the insanity. "This is ridiculous."

"Hey, you're the one that wants to reunite with Team Orange."

"I know, I know. But I thought it would be at a courier outpost or something, not at the epicenter of a religious war with nuclear implications."

"Beggars, choosers."

"C'mon, there's got to be a different angle."

"We can always cycle through another round of wakey punching."

"No, no, no, that was quite enough." Max groaned like a flustered student who had grossly underestimated the exam difficulty. She sighed, grunted, sighed again, grunt-sighed, then flailed her arms. "Fine. Let's do this."

"First things first. Computer!"

"Aye, matey," the computer said, sounding like a raspy pirate.

"Max needs a noodle boost."

"Aye."

Max raised an eyebrow. "What, like a boner pill? Not to point out the obvious, but ..."

Ross scoffed at the human. "No, dumbass. Noodle as in *brain*. It's a concentrated neural kick. Pilots use them in the black to stay alert from port to port."

"Sounds illegal."

"This is space, not Kansas."

The console pinged and opened a small compartment. A braided metal tube slithered out and snaked its way over to Max, causing her to recoil. A conical head reared up to face its target, like a coiled cobra ready to strike. It split into three separate pieces, forming a shiny flower with a spiked pistil at the center.

Max froze and held her breath. "Uuuh ..."

The metal serpent crackled with charge, then shot a blue bolt of lightning between her eyes. Max jolted like a cartoon dope with a finger stuck in a light socket. The hit lasted for a few seconds, leaving her with tense muscles and frizzy hair. The device closed and slithered back into its hole.

"How are you feeling?" Ross said.

Max rolled her shoulders. "Pretty damn good, actually. You know that sweet spot right after a second cup of coffee and before a major boss fight?"

Ross cocked an ear back. "No."

"It's like that, only stronger and cleaner."

"Whatever. The take-home here is that you should stay awake well through our rendezvous. We have several jumps ahead of us and I need you online to navigate the mesh. If you need another hit, just ask the computer."

"Aye," it said. "I'll jab ye like a dirty hooker."

Max clapped and grunted with the newfound energy of a pre-match boxer. She grabbed the yoke, entered the next set of coordinates, and initiated the jump drive. A red icon ladder climbed to a peak and pinged green. "Autobots, roll out," she said, then slapped the jump icon.

Ross rolled his eyes as a sliver of purple light consumed the Ripper.

* * *

Another flash of light belched a tiny freighter into the Behemet system. Inside the cockpit, Zoey and Perra shielded their eyes from the hypergiant off in the distance. The star blazed with a fierce brilliance, despite the billions of miles in between. The viewport auto-dimmed and zoomed in for a closer look, reducing the giant orb to a golden disc peppered with sunspots. The computer added a small dot beside the image, denoting the Mulgawat home star as a mind-melting size comparison.

Zoey mouthed an appropriate expletive and thrust the freighter off to the side. A tangled mesh of shackled planets floated into view, like a cluster of gigantic grapes drifting in the black. Perra vocalized an appropriate expletive. Henry leaned in between them and eyed the bonded worlds with his usual dead-eyed indifference. The Terramesh wandered the outer belt as an absurdist tableau, like a *Monty Python* sketch on a galactic scale.

Perra tilted her head. "That's just ... bizarre."

"Uh huh," Zoey said.

They turned to Henry, who responded with a shrug and nodded forward, commanding to get on with it.

Zoey scowled at the brute and returned her attention to the console. She grabbed the yoke and prepped the ship for entry. Perra enabled the beacon scanner and armed the ion cannons as a precaution. She tapped the control panel and rendered a hologram map of the Terramesh with Grondon highlighted in the center. The nav system created a dotted trajectory that snaked through the cluster and out to their current position. Zoey nodded and swiped a palm up the console, igniting the main engines.

The freighter kicked forward with a burst of blue light. As they neared the planetary clump, the blended colors of rock and flora separated into distinct surfaces, some painted with vibrant tropics, others cloaked with the browns of dirt and desert. Many featured the glittering light of cityscapes with glowing bands of traffic and industry.

Zoey guided the ship through a chaos of traffic created by 86 linked planets. The freighter dipped beneath barges, sailed around fleets, and hugged the hulls of large cruisers as it penetrated a jumbled mess of interconnected rock and steel. The domes of terrestrial landscapes floated across the viewport as they descended into the madness. The freighter crested an enormous pillar to reveal the icy pole of Grondon in the distance. The planet stood out in stark contrast to its neighbors, like a snowball in a stone pit. The city planet of Jarovy appeared behind it, belching smog as the toxic heart of the Terramesh. Henry eyed the world with a purposeful stare, not that anyone could tell. Zoey and Perra remained entranced by the frigid landscape of Grondon.

"How is that even possible?" Perra said.

"I have no idea," Zoey said.

"With this much peripheral gravity, the tectonic friction should have melted everything."

"They never released the proprietary tech, so your guess is as good as mine."

"Artificial atmo locks?"

"Maybe. That would explain why our nav system isn't freaking out."

Perra glanced back to Henry. "Anything to add?"

Henry blinked.

"Fascinating."

The cockpit pinged with a hailing signal. Zoey reached overhead and flicked a series of switches, silencing the alert and enabling coms. Perra tapped a blinking icon, allowing the hologram bust of Migg to piece itself together above the console. The ladies recoiled at the sight of a stumpy creature with red skin and a mustache of squirming tentacles. Large yellow eyes returned a blank stare, like a murderous garden gnome come to life. Despite the unsettling intro, he wore a purple button-up shirt with a black bowtie, as if prepped to take their order at some nightmarish restaurant.

"You must be Migg," Zoey said.

Migg ignored her and opted to address Henry. "Blarga bona mee kwang ock."

Henry nodded.

The hologram crackled and disappeared.

Zoey and Perra traded glances, then turned to Henry.

"Uh, care to elaborate?" Zoey said.

Henry blinked.

The nav system pinged with an incoming transmission. Perra shifted her lips and reluctantly accepted, allowing the system to project a hologram grid upon the viewport. A red trajectory line fell to a remote outpost near the pole. Entry protocols scrolled inside a data panel. The beacon silenced itself and all weapons disarmed.

Zoey turned to Henry.

Henry blinked.

She sneered at the wrinkly brute, then grabbed the yoke and locked onto the trajectory. The freighter pushed forward and carved through the Grondon atmosphere. Soon after, a sea of white filled the viewport. Zoey sailed above a rolling cloud bank, lifting fluffy swirls in her wake. As they neared the outpost, she dipped below the clouds and into a raging blizzard. Snow flurries zipped by the viewport as a wash of turbulence shook the hull. Every clunk and whine from the cargo bay puckered lips and needled nerves. The freighter slowed to a comfortable taxi as a port beacon appeared on the viewport grid. Perra covered her chest with both hands and took a needed breath.

Hull thrusters ignited as the vessel lowered into a rocky ravine. About halfway down, the ledge of a jagged outcrop revealed a small port station hidden inside the ravine wall. As little more than a recessed platform, the destination was less than impressive. Zoey picked one of five landing pads and guided the ship inside. Pillars of blue flame stirred up clouds of snow and steam. Landing claws spread wide to grip the icy plane. A gentle thump concluded their arrival. The main engines spun down, leaving them facing a large metal wall inside a cold and desolate landscape.

Zoey turned to Henry. "Now what?"

Henry blinked.

A massive door panel inside the wall started to rise. The landing pad rumbled beneath the ship and started to crawl towards the opening. Zoey sighed and returned her gaze to the viewport, adding an arm cross to convey her irritation. The platform slid into a large holding bay akin to a service hangar. A small fleet of transport shuttles lined the walls, all dinged and dented like a mess of beater trucks. Creatures in purple uniforms scurried around the enclosure, tending to an array of important tasks. Industrial can lights hung from the craggy ceiling, bathing the room with the harsh glow of a midnight road crew.

The landing pad crawled to the center of the enclosure with the freighter perched on top. The bay door lowered to the ground and ended with a loud clunk, sealing the room from the harsh exterior. Zoey and Perra glanced around the hangar with a discreet curiosity. Purple-suited workers paid them no mind as they darted from task to task. Zoey studied them through a narrowed gaze, knowing damn well that a dangerous operation was afoot.

A series of clunks echoed from the cargo bay.

Henry stood from his seat and squeezed his beefy body down the narrow corridor. He popped into the cargo bay and shook off the discomfort. Zoey and Perra followed him inside, but hung back to watch the scene unfold. The brute stepped over to the airlock and tapped the wall panel. The door slid open, revealing Migg on the outside. Or rather, a terrifying demon scalp with creepy yellow eyes. Migg was of a shorter stature, requiring a leap and scamper to enter the ship. Once inside, he saluted Henry and offered a series of hand gestures akin to a nerdy gang sign. Henry returned the gesture, adding a wink and a chest thump.

Zoey studied the nuke crates, then eyed the wall locker that contained their plasma pistols.

Henry caught the glance and tilted his head, as if to say *really? I mean, go ahead and try if you want to. It's not like we're transporting a big ass payload of volatile nuclear boom-booms. Oh wait, that's exactly what we're doing. Are you stupid or just plain reckless?*

Zoey puckered her lips and glanced away.

Migg studied the crate stacks, then waddled over to the open airlock. "Blarga nom bortic!"

Henry stepped aside as an army of red-skinned goblins poured into the ship and surrounded the stacks. One by one, they plucked the crates and dropped them to readied groups who carried them away like a colony of leafcutter ants. The circus-like performance terrified Zoey and Perra. Every toss and catch drew a flinch, cringe, or yelp. Henry stood beside the airlock, watching the acrobatics without the slightest hint of concern. As the final crate exited the ship, Migg offered Henry another nerd salute, then hopped out the airlock.

Perra heeded her weakened knees and collapsed onto a nearby crate. Zoey leaned against the wall and stared at the ceiling, allowing her horrified brain to reboot.

Henry studied the goblin horde as they loaded the crates into transport shuttles. Engines hummed to life as the ships prepped for departure. He fished his comdev from a breast pocket, noted the time, then eyed the distressed Mulgawats. The brute stepped over to the ladies and stared them down with menace and authority.

"Stay here," he said with an emasculate voice that made Mickey Mouse sound like a hardened criminal.

Zoey and Perra met eyes, then burst into laughter.

"Holy shit fiddles, *that* is your voice?" Zoey said.

"He sounds like he snorted a tank of helium," Perra said.

"Dude, you're one note short of a dog whistle."

"It's like he got kicked in the balls and it stuck."

They howled with laughter, streaming tears down their cheeks. Perra hugged her sides as she fell off the crate. Zoey crumpled to her knees and slapped the floor.

Henry clenched his lips, about-faced, and stepped over to the airlock. He dropped to the ground with a heavy thud and the door slid shut, silencing the cackles. The beast closed his eyes and grumbled before venting a roar of frustration, which came out more as a puppy dog wail. The surrounding goblins stopped in their tracks, then burst into laughter.

Henry facepalmed himself.

CHAPTER 9

Jarovy was a giant city as much as it was a planet. Concrete and steel covered every square mile from pole to pole. And much like a city, Jarovy imported everything and created nothing. Thus, the planet housed numerous cultures, many of them rich beyond words. And, by nature of the location, all of them were criminals. Despite this moniker, many of the locals fancied themselves as proper folk. They wore fine linens, ate posh cuisine, and recoiled with a touch of bother whenever a severed head fell from the sky and splattered all over the sidewalk.

Lord Essien had blasted Trevor's noggin from his body and punted it off the terrace of the Varokin tower (now the Moreon monolith). It had fallen 50 stories and exploded on the sidewalk, scaring the hell out of several Jarovy citizens while spraying the area with brains and blood. Not that it mattered much, because this particular head belonged to a Dimathien. All the blood, muck, and bone began to wiggle back to the impact spot, much to the relief a dainty mistress who found her new evening gown suddenly caked in brain goo. Her tuxedo-clad companion watched a hunk of tongue leap from his lapels and bounce upon the pavement before crawling away. His blunt expression never swayed from a mild curiosity because, after all, these things happen.

Soon after, the head reassembled itself and was left to figure out how to return to the body. The owner remained comatose until it did, so it wasn't as if the noggin could ask for a lift. Fifty stories was a difficult climb for a fit Varokin, let alone for a mobile noodle with a mission. And so, driven by its biological determination, the wayward head sprouted a set of spider legs and made for the tower lobby.

It skittered down the busy sidewalk, bonking walls and ankles with its top-heavy mass. Yelps and screams greeted the sight, especially when darting between legs. A lazy-eyed expression and dangling tongue did not help matters much. The fleshy globe rounded a final corner and raced into the tower lobby. Oddly enough, the terrifying creature seemed well-placed inside the stark black interior, as it matched the ominous tone in more ways than one. The white robes of Moreon usurpers filled the lobby. They paid no attention to the wobbling spider head, as Dimathiens were accustomed to such things. However, if any one of them had taken the time to identify the noggin and return it to its owner, they would have likely curried favor from the supreme leader it belonged to.

The ultimate missed opportunity.

The head moseyed through the lobby and arrived at the elevator shafts. It waited for the next available lift behind a group of robed adherents. A sharp ding echoed from above and a pair of tarnished doors slid open. Everyone stepped inside and tapped their desired floors. The head, having no arms and the leg reach of a Chihuahua, aimed some spittle at the top button. It took several tries and some extra floor selections, but he finally hit it.

The ride was anything but pleasant. Occupants tried to ignore the wobbly spider head in the corner, opting to stare straight ahead and nod along to the mundane music. Each stop saw white robes depart without as much as a curious glance. Before long, the head was all by its lonesome. The mishit spittles resulted in a few awkward stops where the elevator dinged and the doors slid open, gifting anyone in the hallway a brief view of a teetering spider head inside an otherwise empty lift. The peculiar sight was very effective at killing conversations.

With a final ding, the elevator arrived at the top floor. The doors slid open and the spider head skittered out onto a black marble floor. It spun right, then left, then right again before coming to the frustrating conclusion that the top floor wasn't actually the top floor. No stairs or subsequent lifts, just a large open room with a round table flanked by pointy chairs, likely a battle planning area where Varokin captains stroked chins and sneered at one another. The upper floors were only accessible by aircraft, a security measure imposed by Lord Essien after an unfortunate pizza delivery mishap. Peeved by the impasse, the creature smacked its face on the floor in the spider-head equivalent of a facepalm.

But alas, life finds a way.

Or rather, life finds an air duct.

The creature spotted an intake vent along the rear wall. It skittered over and pried the cover free, using the wall as leverage. The head entered the duct system and climbed its way to the terrace level, using little more than luck and blind resolve. After several wrong turns and annoying dead ends, it finally found a ceiling vent that emitted the familiar scent of the terrace tunnel. Lacking the aid of a screwdriver (or a hand to twist it for that matter), the creature opted for brute force. It started face-smashing the vent like a schizophrenic lunatic, sending harsh clanks echoing down the tunnel. The cover gave way and the head fell to the metal floor, hitting with a wet smack. A leg broke off, which promptly crawled back and reattached itself. Tasting a well-fought victory, the noggin leapt to its spidery feet and sprinted for the terrace doors.

The creature tore through the passage like a facehugger chasing down the dumbass that poked its egg sack. A pair of black metal panes appeared in the distance with a glowing wall panel off to the side. Using its momentum, the noggin scampered up the adjacent wall like a skateboarder owning a half-pipe. It slapped the panel with a cheek, resulting in a sharp ping. The terrace doors slid open before the creature finished its clumsy tumble back to the floor. Undaunted, it scampered to its feet and skittered out onto the landing pad, only to skid to a halt shortly after.

Lord Essien's jet black shuttle rested with eerie stillness upon the platform. The nonstop Jarovy traffic flowed behind it with the landscapes of neighboring planets filling the sky. The shuttle's black viewports and streamlined frame gave it an ominous presence, like a dozing panther.

And there it was.

Trevor's headless body dangled from the nose cone like a cheap Halloween decoration.

Lord Essien snickered from the comfort of a lawn chair nearby. Jai stood behind her with arms tucked behind his back. She had commanded him to hang the body from the nose of the ship, which he did. It swayed like a ragdoll with a length of rope wrapped around an ankle. A pool of green blood covered the ground beneath it, which never grew or lessened. Drops fell from the neck stump and splashed into the puddle. From there, they slithered over to the landing gear, climbed up the side of the ship, out to the nose, down the rope, and back into the body, only to spill from the neck again. Lord Essien found this incredibly amusing, but not nearly as much as the spider head's strained assessment of how to reattach itself.

With destination in sight, it shook off the frustration and started to tackle the problem. It skittered over to the landing gear, climbed up the metal frame, and managed to reach the nose cone, only to lose its footing on the slippery surface and smack the ground again. Undeterred, the head repeated the attempt over and over and over. Each slip and splat drew a guffaw from Lord Essien, as if watching a cherished sports blooper on endless repeat.

"That's messed up," Jai said.

"The fucker can regenerate. Cry me a river."

The head fell and splat.

"So what's the plan, m'lord?"

"What, you mean besides watching this quality spectacle for hours on end?"

"Affirmative."

"Well, I suppose the next order of business is to appraise the full armada and start manning ships. I need to see what this trash heap can do."

The head fell and splat.

Jai cringed and studied the head as is shook off the latest attempt. "Don't we need *him* for that?"

Essien sighed. "Yeah, I suppose. Go cut him down."

Jai unsheathed a blade and stepped over to the dangling corpse. He severed the rope with a quick swipe, allowing the body to fall into a crumpled pile. The head, now halfway up on its current attempt, abandoned the task and leapt off the ship, smacking the ground one last time. It scrambled to its feet and skittered over to the headless body. Jai shook his head with envy as the spider legs jammed themselves into the neck stump and reset the errant noggin. Moments later, the body stirred with life.

Trevor rubbed his temples while climbing to his feet. He rolled his shoulders and arched his back for a much-needed stretch. Regaining his wits and bearings, he turned towards the tower entrance, putting him face to face with Jai. Trevor yelped and jerked backwards. "Uncool."

"Do you know how goddamn lucky you are?"

Trevor stammered and glanced away, as if confused by the question.

Lord Essien strolled around Jai with hands at her waist. She locked eyes with Trevor and settled into the hip lean of a runway model. "Now that we understand one another, it's time prep for war."

"So soon?" a voice said from behind.

All three turned to the tower entrance where Orantha Nifan stood in her silken robe. An opulent scarf stretched across her forehead and down around her neck, exposing her full face. Strands of white hair disappeared beneath the fabric, pulled tight against her ashen skin. Her cobalt eyes and dark gray lips formed a calm yet shrewd expression, a look tailor-made to goad Lord Essien.

Trevor stiffened his stance. "Identify yourself, stranger. For you are trespassing upon the hallowed property of the mighty Moreon

Emp—"

Essien gnashed her teeth and blasted Trevor in the face, spraying skull goop onto Jai and the shuttle.

Jai sighed as he flicked bits of brain from his suit.

Essien stomped towards Nifan, blasting her with every step. Streaks of plasma zipped through the hologram image and struck the metal doors behind her, raining sparks onto the platform. Nifan maintained her unflinching posture as Essien continued her rage-fueled approach. With a final step and shot, Essien holstered her pistol and crossed her arms in disgust. Impact smoke abated as blast echoes faded into the distance.

"How comically unnecessary," Nifan said in her usual elitist tone.

"Shut up, hooker. I would blast my own minion if they bore a resemblance."

Nifan smirked. "I do tend to bring that out of you."

"Mark my words, bitch. One day I will watch that dainty body explode in front of me."

"Perhaps."

Essien studied the lifelike hologram image from head to toe. "Neat trick, which tells me you're in the vicinity."

"Am I?"

"How else could you manage remote projection?"

"Oh, is that what this is?"

Essien narrowed her eyes.

Nifan moseyed over to a nearby railing and leaned back against the bar.

Essien un-narrowed her eyes. "An even better trick."

"That is your greatest weakness as a Varokin. You balk at technology in favor of bigger booms."

Essien re-narrowed her eyes.

"I extinguished your entire fleet with the aid of a single Suth'ra scientist. Just imagine what I could do if I actually tried." Nifan glanced at the Jarovy cityscape.

"Ah, and the point emerges. You know, you could have just said 'stand down or I will destroy Jarovy' like a proper villain."

"Is that what I'm doing?"

Essien shook her head. "You and your fucking riddles, I swear to Tim."

"Fine." Nifan lifted from the railing and sauntered over to the terrace entrance. "You want a straight answer? Follow me." She turned away and floated into the tunnel.

Essien gripped her waist like a sideline coach pondering a play. She turned to Jai and a newly reformed Trevor, both of whom responded with nervous stares. She gnawed at her cheek and returned her attention to the tunnel, now glowing blue with Nifan's hologram. She exhaled a heavy sigh and waved her hand forward. "Let's go."

She stepped into the dark corridor with Jai and Trevor following close behind. Nifan stood a stone's throw away, studying their cautious approach through an amused smirk. Her presence inside the passageway resembled a ghost in a haunted house, elevating an already palpable dread. Essien clanked to a stop, leaving a few meters of space in between them.

"How do you know my tower?"

"*Your* tower?"

"Don't get cute with me. You know what I mean."

Nifan grinned. "Walk with me."

Essien sighed and stepped forward.

They strolled down the corridor side by side with Nifan setting the pace. The sharp clanks of Essien's boots echoed down the passage. Jai and Trevor remained close by, doing their best to soften their presence. Trevor kept his shoulders tucked and his hands hidden, wearing his fear for all to see. Jai maintained a stiff posture and steady stride as his wary eyes scanned the interior.

"You left me no choice, you know," Nifan said with a somber tone. "You and your Varokin goons were playing in a pool they didn't belong."

"I had every right, same as you."

"No, you didn't. You never did. You never *earned* it."

Essien chuckled in a mocking manner. "As if the Veiled Traders are merit-based."

Nifan shook her head. "Silly girl."

"I staked my claim, just as they did."

"No, you tried to jack an advantageous artifact. Hardly the same thing."

"Since when do you care about precepts?"

"I don't. I only care about competition."

Essien stopped to face Nifan. "So *that's* why you're here. You want to force me out, make sure I never see the inside of another bridge."

Nifan grinned. "In a way, yes."

"In a way, nothing. You—"

"The Varokins were galactic thugs, dear. Not criminals. Eliminating your fleet was a service to the network, not an undercut. You and your merry band of bullies plagued the black for far too long."

"And yet I rebuild."

Nifan sighed. "And yet you rebuild."

Essien took a step forward. "Your treachery was a speed bump, nothing more. I have already forged accords that will expand my leverage tenfold."

"Your influence is a cancer. Especially here."

"So what's the play? You want to hit Jarovy and destroy the tower? You can try, but I already have a shiny new fleet guarding the stronghold."

Nifan chuckled. "You suffer from a deficiency of scale, my sweet. You brace for the small play, but remain blind to the big picture."

Lord Essien sneered and started to respond, but an eerie stillness infected her mind. She glanced at Jai down the tunnel, who stood tall and stiff with a wide-eyed stare. Trevor was gone.

"Where's the moron?" she said.

Jai remained silent and stared straight ahead.

Essien gnashed her teeth and stomped towards Jai. Her heavy heels clanked upon the grated metal. "Hey fuckface, I asked you a question. Where did Trevor run off t—"

Trevor's headless body appeared around a corner.

"It's a trap," Jai said through the corner of his mouth. He fell forward and slammed the ground like a wooden plank. A small dart with red feathering stuck out from the back of his neck.

Essien whipped her gaze back to her nemesis.

Nifan winked.

"Oh, you nasty little cu—"

Henry snatched her head with a black sack and bound her arms and legs before she could muster a fight. A casual yank and toss draped her over his shoulder. Her grunts and kicks failed to register against his stout frame.

"Keep her alert," Nifan said. "I need her to witness the entire thing."

Henry nodded and vanished down an adjacent tunnel.

The hologram faded away.

A cold silence filled the corridor.

Moments later, the moans of a reassembled Trevor broke the dead air. He struggled to his feet, pawing at the wall for balance. Once upright, his sputtering brain started to assess the situation. He gazed down the corridor, uncovering little more than black metal. A subsequent gaze around the corner uncovered the upended feet of Jai Ferenhal. Trevor gasped and shuffled towards the body like a horror movie teen that needs to inspect everything despite a killer on the loose. He dropped to his knees and leaned down to examine the head. Jai stared at the opposite wall with his drooling lips pressed to the floor.

Trevor poked his shoulder.

Jai responded with a wet mumble, like a semi-conscious drunk after a heavy bender.

Trevor sighed. "Thug life is hard."

CHAPTER 10

A lone Ripper ship blinked out of hyperspace several clicks above the Terramesh. Its noodly frame floated in the black like a rusty squid. Inside the cockpit, Max studied the planet cluster as any newcomer did, with mouth agape and eyelids twitching. No sane being could accept the physics-defying image without a bout of mental gymnastics. The transition from *that can't be real* to *holy crap it is* has left many in need of a stiff drink.

Max vocalized the mental sputter as a simple "Whoa." After all, she had grown to expect the unending curveballs the universe lobs from all directions.

"Impressive, eh?" Ross said, still perched on the console like a furry gargoyle.

"How is that even possible?"

"Atmospheric gravity locks, to be grossly simplistic. The designer never released the tech before her company went under. Every planet has its own climatic barrier, which the bridges somehow ignore. Slick as hell, but still unnerving."

"You can say that again."

"But I won't."

"It's just a saying."

"And a really stupid one. How is repeating a statement going to hammer the message home? If I were to *say it again*, would you be prompted for a third round? A fourth? When does a heard and poignant statement lose its relevance and become annoying drivel?"

"Are you done?"

"Never."

"Careful, your gumption is showing."

"You can say that again."

Max glared at the feline, then turned her attention to the scanner output. A few taps created a hologram image of the planetary system. "What's the place again?"

"Grondon."

The hologram pinged in response and faded the exterior planets, revealing a blinking globe underneath. It zoomed inside and brought the targeted world into gridding detail. A sea of chaotic traffic drifted around the barrier. No rhyme or reason, just a patternless swarm of ships floating inside a jumbled mess of planets. A red arrow appeared and blinked near the Grondon pole, denoting their destination. A red line snaked its way through the mesh and back to the Ripper's current position.

Max grinned. "Well that's convenient."

"Your doppelganger has it all mapped out. You're going to rendezvous at the Ferretian base of operations. Zoey and Perra are there right now."

"Doing what? I never took them as crusader types."

"They're not. Nifan forced them into a power play."

"To do what?"

Ross shrugged. "Does it matter?"

Max huffed. "Your detachment is comforting."

"Eye on the prize, lady. Let's get you down there."

Max took a deep breath and gripped the yoke.

"By the way, you're in a stolen Ripper with a silenced beacon. It is one of the few Black Razor ships that survived the battle at Hollow Hold. The Varokins have been usurped inside the Terramesh. In other words, everyone here wants to kill you."

Max closed her eyes and fought a potent urge to punch Ross off the console. She mentally laughed at the image and returned her gaze to the viewport. A swipe and tap ignited the main engine. She took a measured breath, lobbed a stink eye at the feline, then pushed the yoke forward. The Ripper surged towards the mesh on a cone of red flame.

In reality, no one cared.

Due to the close proximity of neighboring worlds, ships inside the Terramesh paid little attention to each other. They were far more concerned with staying alive. One false move could result in a barrier crash or a head-on collision with a massive pylon. In other words, they minded their own damn business. They adhered to the same unspoken rules of rush hour traffic: eyes on the road, keep up with the flow, don't drive like a lunatic.

The Ripper cruised around a desert planet to reveal the snowy expanse of Grondon. A shimmering pillar speared it like a lollipop, fusing fire and ice. Max dove beneath the sky bridge and followed it like a makeshift freeway. Mag-trams sped overhead, shuttling dregs between worlds. As the ship neared Grondon, the crests of mountain ranges appeared as shadowy rivers. They zigzagged across the planet, giving it the facade of a cracked egg. An unforgiving landscape, ideal housing for a covert force.

A hailing signal chirped inside the cockpit. Max reached across the console and tapped a blinking icon. The hologram bust of Migg and his noodly mustache pieced together. He eyed Max, then flutter-spat and turned to Ross.

"Blarga blark," he said.

"Blarga binka," Ross said, adding a nod.

"Blarga bakka gena sheong."

"Blarga lamma bom bom canny."

Migg snorted. "Blarga fresto?"

Ross glanced at Max. "Blarga delo borcheska."

Migg and Ross shared a chuckle, leaving Max perplexed and annoyed.

"Blarga bop ben deka doop," Migg said, then killed the transmission.

Ross started grooming his paw.

An awkward silence filled the cockpit.

"Well?" Max said.

"Well what?" Ross said, pausing mid-lick.

"What'd he say?"

"He said your mother is a whore."

The console pinged with an incoming signal. A panel of nav data appeared and scrolled through a list of protocols. The yoke reset and the autopilot engaged, pitching the ship towards the upper pole. Max crossed her arms and leaned back as the Ripper punched through the atmo-barrier, dove into a mountain pass, and sped towards the hidden outpost. Soon after, the vessel arrived at the ravine cliff and parked itself on one of the landing pads. A bay door opened and the platform crawled inside.

As the ship passed the exterior wall, a familiar freighter came into view. The boxy ship sat in silence as purple-suited resistance fighters darted around the hangar. Max pressed her palms to the viewport and donned a wide smile.

"There it is! They're really here!"

"Mhmm," Ross said.

Max sighed. "Jeez, would it kill you show some delight? The proverbial band is about to get back together and you just shrug it off like a trip to the dry cleaners."

"My cognition spans the multiverse. This exact scenario is playing out for me a quadrillion times over. Fun fact, they actually murder you in several versions. In one, Mulgawats view human flesh as a delicacy and they flash-freeze you for future snacking. In another, the gals are wanted serial killers and blast a hole in your chest for disturbing a rousing game of checkers. In perhaps my favorite, they fill a giant enema with cottage cheese and—"

"I get the idea, thank you Captain Buzzkill."

"Hence my apathy to this normal-ish encounter."

Max glared at the feline. "*Ish?*"

"Don't worry about it. You're probably fine."

She paused for thought. "I can't tell if you're serious or just messing with me."

"That's kind of my shtick."

Max sighed and returned to the viewport. The platform rumbled to a stop, cueing the gleeful yelp and hurried clap of a fangirl scoring front row tickets. Max spun around and sprinted for the airlock, only to skid to a halt with a sudden rush of pain.

"Ow ow ow! Something bit my asshole." She reached into her waistband and hooked a thin strip of fabric. "The hell is this?"

"What, your thong?"

"Wait, *that's* what thongs feel like? Why would anyone do that to themselves?"

The airlock slid open and a tiny red goblin with yellow eyes jumped inside. Max stumbled backwards, then cringed at another bum nibble.

"Blarga berp," Migg said.

"Blarga boo nata notty," Ross said, then dropped from the console and trotted towards the open airlock. He traded a muted chuckle with Migg as he passed.

Max lingered at the airlock, ogling Migg and his squirmy mustache as he flipped through a clipboard of papers.

Migg paused and locked eyes with the human. "Blarga mi mooka!" he said, which Max clearly understood as *get the hell off my ship!*

Max flinched and scrambled out the door.

"Blarga bop yarko," Migg said from inside. A utility belt sailed through the airlock and landed at Max's feet.

Max reached down and grabbed the sleek accessory. The purple leather matched her suit and featured several small compartments. A sturdy holster contained a compact plasma pistol. Max nodded and latched the belt around her waist, completing the image of whatever the hell she was in that particular universe. She hooked her thumbs inside the belt and glanced around the hangar.

A large banner featuring a giant purple ferret holding a banjo hung with pride from the rear wall. Comrades of all shapes and sizes tended to various ships and stations. The roar of preparation filled the bay, gifting Max an odd sense of belonging. She half-expected to see an X-wing stamped with a purple ferret logo.

Max exhaled a heavy breath while snapping her fingers, like a nervous teen building the courage to ask out a crush. She glanced down at Ross and smiled. "You ready?"

"What, like I'm on pins and needles?"

Max ignored the remark, opting to focus on the glorious reunion at hand. She stepped towards the tiny freighter. A sudden onslaught of butterflies infected her stomach.

"So you're just gonna knock and introduce yourself?"

Max twisted her hands over one another. "I don't know. It's not like I planned this out."

"Obviously. The goal was to sneak on the ship, not con your way inside like a magazine salesman."

"And how the hell would I manage that with everyone running around? I'm the only human here, from what I can gather. Not exactly inconspicuous."

"Suit yourself. Who am I to block a thoroughly amusing confrontation?"

Max clenched her lips.

A short hike later, she arrived at the airlock door of the familiar freighter. Max stared at the pane for what seemed like an eternity as the events of the previous day replayed in her head. She had snuck into a Yarnwal camp, repaired a Ripper, beheaded a dinosaur, escaped Yankar, and crossed the great black sea for this very moment, but recoiled at the thought of rejection. A rush of insecurity infected her mind, like a nerdy kid at the edge of a dance floor. Ross sensed the anxiety and decided to toss her a bone.

"You've earned it," he said. "Go ahead."

Max grinned. "Thanks, buddy." She raised a confident fist and knocked.

The airlock slid open moments later, revealing Zoey in her usual pilot garb. Her choppy black hair and sunburst complexion flooded Max with relief. That is, until her face tightened with rage. Zoey seized Max by the lapels, yanked her inside, and slammed her back against the wall.

"How did you find us?!" Zoey said.

Max stammered in response, adding widened eyes and a mousy whimper.

"Calm down," Ross said as he leapt into the ship. "We're all on the same side here."

"Same side?" Perra said as she emerged from the engine room. Her punky attire and long auburn hair lifted a brief grin on Max's face. She tossed a dirty rag aside and grabbed a monkey wrench, clutching it like a nightstick. "Last time I checked, Maxine was a member of the Veiled Traders."

"Well, yeah, but—"

"But nothing," Zoey said, still pinning Max to the wall. "That little *incident* at the Paxton Mines nearly killed us."

Max shifted her gaze between the ladies. "Sorry?"

"Oh, you're going to be," Perra said as she smacked the wrench into her palm.

A body flew through the airlock and thumped the cargo bay floor, startling everyone inside. The prisoner grunted on impact, then barked an array of curses through a cloth bag. Henry climbed into the vessel soon after. He stood tall and dusted himself off before heeding the current predicament. The group froze, leaving the dull roar of hangar activity and the squirms of a mystery captive. Henry met eyes with Zoey, who leaned into the chest of a frightened Earthling. Without moving his noggin, he glanced at a wrench-wielding Perra, then down to a disinterested house cat.

Perra eyed the prisoner. "Um, who's that?"

Henry thumped the wall panel, closing the airlock door. He stepped over to the captive, hooked her uniform collar, and yanked her to her feet. She stumbled a bit and regained her balance. The energy shackles around her arms and legs crackled with static. Henry glanced around the room, as if prepping for a magic trick. He pinched the black sack and jerked it free, revealing the teardrop skull and silver eyes of Lord Essien.

Everyone gasped, except for Ross, who batted at a piece of lint trapped in the floor grates.

Zoey released Max, who ugly-tumbled to the floor and scrambled back to her feet.

Perra's face had traded worry for an outright shock.

Lord Essien tossed a hateful gaze at Henry, then glanced around the room. She scowled at Perra, sneered at Zoey, and scoffed at Ross. When she got to Max, a sly smile stretched across her face. "Been a while, Maxine."

Max glared at Ross. "Of course she knows me."

Ross snort-chuckled.

"Still raw about the Paxton Mines, I see," Essien said to Zoey. "I'm surprised you haven't killed the bitch after what she did."

"Under *your* orders."

"Her hand, her massacre."

Max raised her hand, drawing the group's attention. "I thought I was a ferret-worshiping freedom fighter."

Essien huffed. "Your treachery knows no bounds."

Max glared at Ross again, who fought hard to restrain an onrush of merriment.

Henry stepped into the center, killing the conversation. He locked eyes with Zoey and nodded towards the cockpit. She sighed and motioned for Perra to join her. They strolled by the group and up the narrow passage, tossing dirty looks to Essien as they passed. Max followed them out of habit.

"Maxine, my darling," Essien said as she stepped by.

Max slowed to a stop and met eyes with the black-lipped battle lord.

Essien grinned, then lunged forward and snatched the plasma pistol from Max's holster. Max yelped and fumbled at the intrusion, drawing the attention of Zoey and Perra in the cockpit. Lord Essien hopped aside and aimed the pistol at Henry, gripping it with shackled hands. He stared back through an expressionless face as he raised his meaty palms into the air. Max slowly backed away with her arms raised. Zoey and Perra rushed to the cargo bay, only to face down the barrel of Lord Essien's pistol. Their hands rose as well, completing the set. The energy braids painted Essien's taut face with a blue sheen. She aimed the pistol at Henry.

"You can take these off now," she said.

Henry stared at her, cold and silent.

Essien fired a shot that zipped by his head and slammed into the airlock door, causing everyone to flinch but Henry. Sparks rained from the impact, many of which bounced off Henry's head and shoulders.

"I'm sorry, did you mistake that for a request?"

Henry expelled a slow sigh and glanced away for a split second, his version of screaming *goddamnit* at the top of his lungs. "Rojan pyek," he said in his nasally mouse-like voice.

The shackles crackled away, but not before Lord Essien burst into laughter. Her toothy howls broke the tension for a moment, prompting everyone else to snort and snicker. She concluded the chuckle with a heavy sigh. "Tim help me, no wonder you're the silent type."

Henry ignored her and stared straight ahead, opting to give a distant wall locker his undivided attention.

Essien gripped the weapon with a free hand and slipped the other inside a breast pocket, retrieving her comdev. She tapped a command without breaking eye contact. The device pinged with acquisition.

"Yersh, herm mmer ... mmerlerd," Jai said.

Essien scrunched her brow and glanced at the comdev. "The hell is wrong with you?"

"Serrr ... erm ..."

"Sweet mercy, gimme that," Trevor said from off-screen. The image jerked and jostled as he wrestled the device away from Jai. "Yes, hi, this is Trevor. Jai is still a bit woozy from the tranq dart. What can I do you for?"

Essien grimaced. "I need you to trace my signal."

Silence responded.

She sighed and glanced around the cargo bay with mild embarrassment. "Well?"

"Yeah, um ... I don't know how to do that," Trevor said in a sheepish tone.

"Geeer mer der ffff ... feern," Jai said from afar.

"You're too drunk, shut up."

"Erm nert."

A muffled scuffle commenced, filling the room with the tinny sounds of children fighting over a toy. Essien pursed her lips and shook her head like a disgruntled grade school teacher. The rest of the group traded bored glances. After a bout of bonks and bellows, the image stabilized on Trevor's lumpy noggin.

"Grondon, Section 14, northern pot roast."

"Eerperst!" Jai said from afar.

"Outpost, sorry."

"Summon all fighters to my location," Essien said.

Silence responded.

Essien grumbled. "Do you copy?"

"Are those the big ones or the little ones?"

"Holy fucknuts, Trevor! Call up anything with a big ass gun and come get me!"

Silence responded.

"We need to work on your people skills," he said, then tossed the comdev to Jai.

"Yersh, m'lerd. Rert awer."

Essien killed the feed and shoved the comdev back into her breast pocket. Everyone else wandered their gazes like bored employees enduring a pointless staff meeting. Henry remained the exception, keeping every muscle braced while continuing his intense examination of a wall locker. Essien glanced around the group, studying clothes and curves to pass the time. While admiring Perra's sassy kicks, her eyes suddenly widened.

"Wait, where's the cat?"

The pistol in her hand exploded.

She recoiled and stumbled backwards.

Everyone turned to Ross, now sitting upon a crate stack beside an open locker. The barrel of a plasma pistol smoked beneath his legs with a paw resting on the trigger.

"Took you long enough," he said. "I was starting to lose hope for a dramatic reveal."

Henry locked eyes with Essien and lowered his arms.

She groaned and glanced away. "Fuck all of you right in the neck."

CHAPTER 11

A mishmash of shuttles and fighters screamed through the Grondon atmosphere, leaving trails of black smoke in their wakes. To the untrained eye, one would have thought that a trash barge had exploded in orbit, vomiting rubbish all over the planet. To the trained eye, the exact same image applied. The Moreon fleet was many things, but pleasant it was not. However, what it lacked in aesthetic appeal, it made up for in firepower.

Back inside the Ferretian outpost, sirens roared over a frenzy of activity. Racks of rifles and munitions emptied as crews prepared for battle. The nuke shuttles had long since departed and the few remaining fighters scrambled to arm their vessels.

The tiny freighter rested on the leftmost of five landing pads. Migg stood outside in the chaos, barking instructions into the open airlock. His tentacle mustache bounced and bobbled as he gestured at the large bay doors. Henry stood just inside the ship, nodding intently at the tiny red goblin. Migg's face flushed with mounting tension, not that anyone could tell. With a final nod and salute, Henry thumped the wall panel and the airlock door slid closed.

Inside, Lord Essien stood with her back to a vertical pipe and wrists bound behind it. She glared at anyone who dared to wander by. Henry moseyed over and double-checked the restraints. Satisfied, he stepped to her front and gave her a quick visual inspection.

Essien raised her chin and glowered at the brute. "Listen well, you loathsome beast. If you think for one second that you can—"

Henry slapped her across the cheek with zero emotion, leaving her in stunned silence. He bagged her head, honked her nose, and walked away.

Up in the cockpit, Zoey and Perra hurried through the launch prep. The console pinged and chirped under blurred hands. The hum of building power filled the ship.

"All systems online," Perra said.

"Gravy," Zoey said.

Henry squeezed his body through the narrow passage, creating the sound of a damp cloth on glass. He popped into the cockpit and settled into the wall seat behind Zoey. As always, his detached expression failed to match the current tone of the predicament. "When that bay door opens, ignite to full thrust and drop into the ravine. Pick a direction and hug the riverbed until we are out of danger."

Perra snorted, then frowned in shame. "I am so sorry, I shouldn't make fun. Your voice is sweet and pleasant, like a squeaky lamb."

Zoey snorted.

Henry eyed them both without moving his head.

"And what about Max and the cat?" Zoey said, turning to the human and feline in the wall seat behind Perra. "Are we really taking these fools to Nifan?"

Henry nodded.

Zoey sighed and glared at Max. "So you twiddled Essien and now you're tonguing Nifan?"

Max shrugged while wearing a cheeky grin. "I have no idea what you're talking about."

"Then why are you smiling like a jackass?"

"I'm just so damn happy to be here right now."

Ross snored in her lap.

Zoey tossed Perra a wary glance, then grabbed the yoke and focused on the bay door through the viewport.

Perra folded her hands and gazed out a side window.

A fighter ship hovered atop pillars of blue flame before coming to a rest upon the adjacent platform. Landing claws pressed the surface as thrusters reduced to an idle hue. The ship resembled a jagged tuning fork, its smoky gray exterior more grimy than polished. A pair of plasma cannons poked through the nose tips, leading back to a round and opaque cockpit. Two more fighters floated to a rest on the far right pads, leaving the center platform empty. They all faced the bay doors, primed for assault. With the vessels in place, the hangar crew scurried behind makeshift barriers. One final ship hovered up from a maintenance shaft and settled upon the central pad.

The sight stole a breath from Perra's lungs.

* * *

A dozen Moreon ships hovered inside the ravine with cannons and missiles locked onto the bay doors. The blocky troop resembled a chorus line of shipping containers armed with heavy artillery. They formed a wide arch around the hangar, cutting off any possible escape. The center ship was by far the most attractive of the bunch. As little more than a stumpy triangle with mismatched paneling, it at least made sense from a symmetrical perspective. Behind the scratched viewport, Trevor and Jai filled a pair of tattered pilot seats. Trevor studied the outpost with an erect posture, trying his best not to look like a frightened child. Jai remained a robust presence, despite the puffy eyes and drool stains.

Trevor tapped the console, requesting a comlink with the rebel base. Moments later, the hologram bust of Migg pieced itself together. A tense silence infected the cockpit as Trevor brain-fumbled through negotiation protocols. Large yellow eyes stared back at him. Migg and his wriggling mustache remained poised and silent. Trevor stammered a bit before finding a reasonable collection of words.

"Rebel General of the Ferretian Force," he said.

"Blarga garp," Migg said.

Trevor opened his mouth to respond, then turned to his co-pilot. Jai stared straight ahead and grunted as a bead of drool abandoned his lip.

"Um ..." Trevor glanced between the two, then stiffened his chin and focused on Migg. "You have our leader captive and we would like her back. You are to release Lord Essien or the mighty Moreons will ... will rain a righteous waterfall of rampage and dismay and nasty smoke destruction chaos with explosive sorrow upon thy fort."

Jai closed his eyes and shook his head.

"Blarga koo morp." Migg nodded and the transmission blinked away.

A restive silence filled the cockpit.

"What happened?" Trevor said. "Did we win?"

Jai responded with a sleepy-eyed groan.

The center bay door unlocked and started to open.

Trevor turned to Jai and donned a cheeky grin, basking in his newfound status as a shrewd negotiator. He exhaled a victory sigh and returned a cocky gaze to the door, only to stare into the face of a battle-ready Ripper. The nightmarish glare of its tentacle arsenal bathed the platform in a bloody sheen. The arms expanded into a burning flower of death. Inside the cockpit, Migg gripped the yoke with his tiny red hands. A sinister grin crept across his face as he jammed his thumbs into the cannon triggers.

Jai shrieked like a terror-struck toddler and snatched the yoke from Trevor's hands. He yanked it off to the side and the ship barreled away as a hail of plasma streaks slammed into the ravine wall behind them.

Migg thrust the Ripper out of the hangar and proceeded to shred his way through the Moreon ships. Three of them exploded before he even cleared the platform. Flashes and thunder filled the ravine as the Ripper unleashed its deadly torrent. The Moreon ships scattered to engage, prompting the other doors to rise and release the rebel fighters. Trevor and Jai watched from the ravine floor as the Ripper and its winged assassins decimated their precious fleet. A fresh lot of Moreon fighters sliced through the atmo-barrier on their way to assist. Migg and his posse raced towards them as the fiery guts of the first squad showered into the ravine.

* * *

The final bay door opened.

Zoey swiped the thrusters to full power and flamed the freighter out of the hangar. It dipped over the platform edge and dove into the ravine. After a sharp descent, the vessel slowed to a hover above the riverbed, sending ripples to the shores. Zoey ignited the main engines and kicked the vessel forward, lifting an arch of water in her wake.

* * *

Trevor, fresh off a panic attack, pointed at the freighter racing into the distance. "There they are! Let's get 'em!"

Jai lifted an eyebrow and opened his palm, drunk-speak for *you're in the pilot seat, dumbass.*

"Ah, yes." Trevor gripped the yoke, flamed the engines, and thrust forward in pursuit. The clunky ship followed the freighter's wake, lifting a water arch of its own.

* * *

Zoey steered the ship around craggy corners and sailed over rumbling rapids. The full burn of the twin rear engines reflected off the white walls of the ravine, creating a bright red halo that raced alongside. With the outpost long behind them, she slowed the vessel to a reasonable pace. A hailing ping echoed overhead. Perra tapped the console, lifting the hologram bust of Nifan.

"Hello, ladies," Nifan said.

"Nifan," Zoey said with an insolent tone, as if to greet a telemarketer.

Nifan grinned, then eyed Henry. "Package secure?"

Henry nodded.

"Yeah, about that package," Zoey said. "You do know that having her on this ship makes us the biggest target in the Terramesh, right?"

Nifan shrugged. "Then don't tell anyone."

"She already informed the entire Moreon fleet."

"And how did she do that?"

"She snatched a plasma pistol from your other package and held us up."

Max leaned into view and waved. "Hi!"

Nifan winked at Max, then turned back to Zoey. "Well, it seems that you have the situation under control."

"Yeah, thanks to a feline ex machina."

"Wha—what?"

"Doesn't matter. What *does* matter is that you're using a standard comlink, which means you're in range."

"Correct. My ship is currently in orbit above Kurm. Exit the mesh there and await further instruction."

"And what if—"

Nifan killed the transmission, leaving Zoey to huff and swallow the reply.

Perra tapped the console, creating a hologram rendition of the Terramesh. "Kurm." An outer planet blinked and the rest faded away. The nav system drew a red line from the current location to the target. "Well, at least it's nearby. We can exit along the—"

A plasma streak zipped by the viewport and slammed into the riverbed, rumbling the hull and spraying the ship with icy water. Max screamed like a skittish schoolgirl. The jostle yanked Ross from his catnap, but he grumbled some curses and fell back asleep. Zoey and Perra flinched twice, once for the blast, and once for the resulting scream. Henry maintained his *too cool to care about death* demeanor. Lord Essien yelped from the back and started shout-cursing in a very unsavory language.

"Hold onto something!" Zoey thumped the console.

The main engines exploded with thrust, hurling the tiny freighter down the ravine.

* * *

Trevor and Jai tracked the ship from above, stalking the upper ledge. With the chase on, they plunged to the riverbed and surged forward with a burst of flame.

"We had them target locked," Trevor said. "How in the wide world of heck did you miss that shot?"

Jai cradled the co-pilot yoke with both arms, using it for balance. His head bobbled like a tilt-a-whirl victim getting ready to vomit. "Essien inside," he said, opting for the lean grammar of a throbbing hangover. "Warning shot. Hit when needed."

"That makes no sense."

Jai sighed. "Battle strat. Need support. Omen danger. No dogfight. Force mistake. Moron."

"Moreon."

"No misspeak."

* * *

Zoey sailed under cliffs and hugged outcrops, hoping to lose the pursuers. Trevor managed to keep up, albeit clumsy and ungraceful. He banged and scraped the hull with every sharp turn, raining sparks and the occasional panel into the ravine. Trevor cringed with every impact, like a rookie racer misjudging the track. Jai focused on a patch of rocky nodes ahead of the freighter. He fired into them, showering the path with jagged boulders. Zoey avoided them all, dipping and diving like a dodgeball pro.

"They're missing us on purpose," Perra said.

"As if I would let them hit us," Zoey said.

"Not what I meant. Watch the impact angles. All the hits are intentional and peripheral."

Zoey dropped the throttle and steered the vessel around a tight corner, pressing everyone into their seats. "Little busy at the moment."

"They're not going to risk killing Essien, which gives us the upper hand." Perra tapped the console, creating a grid of beacon activity in the immediate vicinity. A blue dot raced through the ravine outline, denoting their current position. A single red dot followed close behind. "See, just one ship. You could easily take them."

"Not an option. Can't risk the package on a dogfight."

"We're already in a dogfight. Can we not—"

"Rambo 2!" Max said.

Everyone, including Henry, turned to the human.

Max clapped like an excitable fangirl. "Let's do a Rambo 2! Any of you see that flick?"

Zoey scrunched her brow. "What in Tim's name are you blathering about?"

Another plasma streak zipped by and slammed into an outcrop, severing a giant sheet of rock. The monolith hit the ravine floor and started falling across the river. Zoey barrel-rolled to the opposite side, narrowly evading the crash and churning every stomach in the ship. Lord Essien resumed her cursing from the cargo bay.

Perra turned to Max. "Explain."

"Okay, it's really simple, but in a really hard and tricky kind of way."

"That's not as reassuring as you think it is."

"First, we need to widen the gap, get as much distance as we can between us and them. Find a large open area inside the ravine system. Henry, grab your comdev. This is going to take some coordination."

Henry offered a scant smirk and reached into his breast pocket. Zoey rounded a bend and swiped the engines to full throttle. The freighter surged forward, flashing through the canyon and escaping the target range.

*   *   *

"Darn it all to heck and back," Trevor said. He thumped the console with the ferocity of a pouty infant, then frowned and folded his hands. "Pardon my violent outburst. It was distasteful and I apologize."

Jai chose not to respond, opting to brain-sigh instead.

"Computer, re-acquire target lock."

"Unable," the computer said, using the monotone voice of an 80's era robot.

"Why not?"

"Range."

"Huh? What about range?"

"Out."

"What about missile lock?"

"Unable."

"Why not?"

"Terrain."

Trevor huffed. "Okay, what else we got?"

"Stuff."

"What kind of stuff?"

"Snacks."

"Thank you, but I had a large lunch."

"Drinks."

"Um, hardly the time to tie one on. And besides, I am a Moreon. My faith forbids me from imbibing substances that alter my awareness. I need to remain crisp and clear-headed for divine worship."

The computer paused before responding. "Cool."

Trevor turned to Jai. "I can't tell, was that sarcastic?"

Jai responded with a flaccid expression that sucked any and all regard from his associate. He inhaled a deep breath, slapped himself across the cheek several times, then expelled a grumbling moan. He climbed to his feet, shuffled over to Trevor, and loomed over him like a hungry yeti.

Trevor recoiled. "Um, what are you—"

Jai snatched him by the shoulders and tossed him into the other seat, having expended his daily allotment of fucks to give. Trevor yelped on impact and started to fuss, but the brute vaporized any retort with a bloodshot death stare. Jai plopped into the pilot chair, grabbed the yoke, and shook his noggin to clear some brain space.

"Computer, run a beacon scan for all vessels inside a 20 mark radius. Isolate M-class freighters and highlight vitals on the navigation grid."

"Affirmative."

A hologram grid of the ravine system spread across the viewport. The system zoomed out to an aerial view of the requested radius with the current area highlighted. Several icons appeared, along with panels of class and distance info. One of them morphed into a red X, denoting the freighter's position inside an outlying basin.

Jai slogged his gaze over to Trevor.

"You're so good at this," Trevor said, adding the peppy grin of a camp counselor.

Jai shook his head like a disillusioned parent. He blazed the engines and yanked the yoke off to the side. The ship cut hard into a narrow channel, pressing them to the seats. The navigation grid guided them through a rocky maze of twists and turns. Trevor squirmed at the aggressive flying, adding the occasional yelp as the ship carved around tight corners.

With a final turn and burn, the ship sailed by the upper ridge of a broad basin. The river spread into a shallow lake before flowing into the next canyon in the distance. Dense shrubs and round boulders lined the shore, all dusted with snow. Towering cliffs encircled the valley, creating a grand bowl inside the white landscape. Near the center, the tiny freighter rested atop a rocky reef, facing the oncoming ship. The engines emitted thin lines of smoke, as if overheated or disabled.

Jai slowed the vessel to a cautious hover above the lake, putting them a stone's throw away. Hull thrusters pushed waves to the shores as clouds of steam swirled around the ship. Jai studied the peculiar sight through narrowed eyes, unable to make sense of the situation. Panel data showed no armed weapons or target locks. He tried to establish coms, but the freighter failed to respond. A heavy sigh escaped his lungs as he crossed his arms and grunted with confusion.

"Maybe Lord Essien retook the ship," Trevor said.

"Against The Omen and a Boobybork?"

Trevor snorted, then immediately deflated. "Forgive me. My faith forbids me from public displays of amusement."

Jai huffed. "You are bondage incarnate."

"We prefer the term *enlightened.*"

"Hmph. One day you will have to explain to me how regression equals wisdom."

A dull hum hooked both of their attentions. Jai glanced around the cockpit as Trevor gazed out the viewport. The hum grew louder and louder, but the freighter out in front remained still and unresponsive.

Trevor scratched one of his chin lumps. "Where is that coming fr—"

Jai raised a hand, motioning for silence. He studied the ceiling with mouth agape. "I know that sound."

The hum morphed into a damp roar.

Jai ruffled his brow, but then his eyes popped open with a horrifying realization. "Fuck!"

SLUNK! The ear-splitting sound of a giant sword swipe jostled the hull. The vessel whined for a moment, then split in two and splashed into the lake, tossing Jai and Trevor to the floor. The nose and tail sections thumped the lakebed a few meters down, flooding the interior with icy water.

Jai grabbed Trevor and scrambled out of the cockpit as Migg and his Ripper circled around for another attack. He sloshed into a swamped cargo hold, now cleaved down the center with surgical precision. Jai and Trevor dove into the churning water and swam for their lives. As they neared the shore, Migg rained hellfire onto the wrecked vessel, which exploded into a ball of flame.

* * *

Zoey and Perra wore stunned expressions as columns of black smoke raised from the flaming wreckage.

Max pumped her fists and cheered. "Yeah! Take *that* you dirty Russian!"

Henry glanced at Max and raised a fist.

Max bumped it, adding a finger explosion.

Henry lowered his unexploded fist.

Perra nodded slowly. "That was ... oddly effective. Why have we never heard of the Rambo maneuver?"

"Covert ops, I imagine." Zoey turned to Max. "Did the Veiled Traders teach you that?"

"No. Cinemax."

Zoey nodded, then established a comlink to Migg.

The hologram bust of a red goblin pieced together above the console. "Blarga boom boom."

Henry nodded his thanks.

"Blarga nym bogin," Migg said, then offered a Ferretian salute and killed the feed.

The Ripper retracted its arsenal and soared into the sky upon a pillar of red flame. Henry nudged Zoey and pointed to the departing ship, instructing her to follow. She nodded and ignited the thrusters. The freighter lifted from a rocky patch and hovered above the lake, curling clouds of steam around the frame. The main engines blazed to life and the freighter surged skyward.

* * *

Jai and Trevor crawled out of the icy water and onto an equally icy shoreline. A hard shiver set in as they climbed to their feet and glanced around the snowy basin. Biting winds needled their skins through sodden clothes. A flaming pile of wreckage poked through the lake, creating a tiny island of sadness and regret. Trevor held out his open palms, as if to siphon heat from the distant flames.

"Well, I guess we could huddle together for warmth or something," Trevor said through chattering teeth. "Unless, of course, you have a better idea."

Jai paused for thought, then unsheathed a large dagger and turned to Trevor.

CHAPTER 12

The Ripper and freighter tore through the atmo-barrier of Grondon, departing the white planet and entering the heart of the Terramesh. The cityscape of Jarovy gleamed off in the distance. The domes of neighboring realms filled the void in all directions with icy poles, stark deserts, and lush jungles. Commerce centers sparkled inside sprawling valleys. Island chains peppered giant oceans. Every globe connected to the next, creating an endless maze of dirt and steel.

Migg surged forward, steering the Ripper into the open space between Grondon and its neighbor. Zoey boosted the engines in order to keep pace. They sailed around enormous sky bridges and weaved through chaotic traffic. No one gave them a second look as the old Varokin fighter buzzed about the colossal labyrinth with a dirty dumpster in tow.

Migg zipped through a shuttle convoy and barrel-rolled around a lumbering barge, forcing Zoey to dive underneath and reunite on the other side. She grunted and gnashed her teeth as she tried to match the maneuvers. Every so often, the acrobatics drew a grin of admiration.

"Wow. Migg is a hell of a pilot."

"That he is," Perra said.

Max gripped her harness with both hands while ogling the viewport. She wore a cheeky grin as if enjoying the hell out of a flight simulator.

Ross continued to nap on her lap with claws dug into her leather pants for support.

Lord Essien grumbled from the cargo bay, emitting the occasional yelp-curse combo.

Henry maintained his statuesque presence. That is, until a long-held camaraderie bubbled from the depths. "Migg is an exceptional pilot."

Zoey raised her brow with curiosity.

Perra and Max turned to the wrinkled brute.

Henry closed his eyes and took a weighted breath, as if to prep for a round of meditation. "We fought side by side during the Larroko Raid of Kyvon Rai. We were both grunts at the time, little more than expendable meat, but he had my back despite being a filthy Durflock.

"I shouldered a seething hatred for most of my life. We were taught from an early age to despise their race as part of a severe indoctrination. Hate for the sake of hate, a diet of pure tribal animus. We abhorred their culture, their nature, their beliefs, everything. Typical 'us versus them' mentality. We worshiped a shiny rock, they worshiped a purple ferret, and we hated them for it. We were tall with pink skin, they were short with red skin, and we hated them for it. The hate festered inside us with the full capacity of our being.

"Our planets warred for centuries over trivial contrasts. The deaths were innumerable and the scars never healed. I donned the blood of my brethren more times than I care to recall. I vowed to slit a Durflock throat for every brother and sister I lost. And I succeeded, many times over. I know what Durflock blood tastes like. It's warm and thick and metallic. It makes me think of rusty sap on a summer dawn. They're tough to kill and their blood runs as red as their skin, so you never knew who was close to death. They fought and flailed to the bitter end like rabid animals, using their own hatred as a fiery fuel.

"But then came the Larrokos.

"The Boobyborks and Durflocks fought a never-ending war. Entire generations grew up knowing nothing but spite and woe. But when something as malignant as the Larrokos enter the fray, you start to question the potency of your own venom. They showed us a level of cruelty that we were not prepared to see. The depths of their evil rattled our world in ways we never could have imagined. When the first wave hit, it left us all in a state of paralysis. Boobybork, Durflock, didn't matter. We had gazed into the eyes of true villainy, wickedness on an unimaginable scale. We found peace in a chamber of horrors and united under a banner of fear. The Larrokos shredded the veils of prejudice and awakened us to the depravities of an uncaring universe. I dare not speak them aloud, for the depictions would scar your minds with madness.

"The first wave induced a systematic slaughter that cut our populations in half. The next wave took another half, then another, onward into a callous oblivion. As we stared into the dark void of extinction, one of our scouting groups uncovered a valuable weakness. The Larrokos were a hive mind. They shared a neural bond controlled by a nefarious queen. Our concerted mission had simplified. Kill the queen and live. Fail and perish.

"Further recons pinpointed the queen on Kyvon Rai, a rocky moon orbiting a gas giant on the outskirts of our own system. The breathable air and dense ecosystem made it an ideal place to hide, but a terrible place to battle. Regardless, we needed to end their rot.

"Our united force was no match for the Larrokos on an open plane. We all knew that any attack on Kyvon Rai was likely a one-way ticket. The assault needed to be sublime, a divine coordination, a singular strike the likes of which had never been seen and would never be seen again. And so, our leaders got to work.

"We trained day and night. Every boob, bork, and binky had a role to play. What we had in strength, the Durflocks matched in rigor. Their pilots and assassins were unrivaled, so they led our assault squads. I was a scrapper, a ground soldier who was good with a blade. Migg was my pilot. We met on the training grounds. We established a foundation of respect that grew into admiration and eventually friendship. We thought alike. We dissected strategy with a single mind. Migg knew how to leverage me in a tight situation. He also knew that I had his back.

"When raid day came, I was frightened. Not about the battle, but about losing what we had built. Migg was my brother and the thought of losing him infected my psyche with a caustic dread. We were not going to lose this battle. I would fight the entire hive alone if I had to. And for a time, I did. I could think of nothing else.

"We descended on Kyvon Rai like flaming rain. Streaks of red and orange pierced the clouds as our mighty armada fell with a single purpose. Migg's shuttle sliced through the heavens with two dozen grunts inside. I manned a cannon mount, an ionic blaster with copious throughput. I can still feel the rushing wind on my face. The air smelled crisp and verdant, like dried moss.

"The battle started before our feet touched the ground. Red streaks zipped by the vessel, the heated laser blasts of ground cannons. Migg evaded every shot on his way down. The shuttle banked and swerved like a hawk on the wing. The metal beast was an extension of himself, in a very real sense. It gave us a tangible sense of safety and security, and to a point, invincibility.

"As we neared the surface, I could trace the outlines of Larroko watchtowers. I opened fire, unleashing a torrent of ion pulses. Several towers exploded on impact. Others took blasts to their trusses and crumbled into to the surrounding thickets. The lush landscape of Kyvon Rai soon found itself painted with a yellow sheen. We set the entire moon on fire. From orbit, the world looked diseased, as if choked by the creeping tendrils of death.

"The shuttles grouped inside an open valley to offload troops. Soldiers poured into the grass like a rush of surging water. I remained behind the cannon to cover Migg on his return to orbit. Each transport carrier was tasked to deliver three payloads of personnel. Some gathered more because others never returned. I wish I could say that Migg fulfilled his end of the bargain. And in a way, he did.

"As transports returned to orbit, the Larrokos launched interceptor rockets. The majority of our ship losses came in this manner. The laser blasts crippled and maimed, but the guided missiles rarely missed their mark. Luckily, our fleet greatly outnumbered their launchers. By the sheer grace of math, most of our shuttles completed their missions.

"Migg lifted his shuttle from the valley floor and began his second run, cognizant of missiles turning his neighbors into balls of flame. I resumed my tower assault as the main engines ignited and pushed us skyward.

"And then I saw it.

"A white exhaust trail emerged from a nearby patch of jungle. The missile screamed towards us, but no alarm had sounded. It had locked onto another ship ahead of us. I tried to shoot it down, but the risk of hitting other ships was too great. I could only fire short bursts, all of which missed. The missile continued its deadly hunt.

"Migg was thrust into the corner of a dreadful dilemma. On one hand, he could watch the missile scream by and hit its target, a rookie pilot with dubious skill. Certain death for the greenhorn and his gunner, but guaranteed passage back to the cruiser to shuttle more soldiers. Or, he could swerve into the trajectory and force it to hit a seasoned pilot with a greater chance of survival.

"It was an easy decision.

"Migg barrel-rolled behind the rookie pilot. The missile slammed into our tail section and exploded on impact. The deafening blast destroyed the stern and swallowed us in a cloud of fire. I clutched the cannon for dear life as the ship plummeted towards the surface. Migg struggled to control the crippled vessel. Flames poured from the fuselage behind me. When you stare into a wall of hellfire, you welcome the sweet release of death. I braced for impact, wondering if I would meet my fate with charred flesh.

"The transport spun for an eternity, creating a swirling inferno. But then, much to my astonishment, the ship leveled out into a comfortable glide. Migg had managed to correct the fall with a combination of functional hull thrusters and manual drag maneuvers. We drifted on crippled wings and crash-landed into a patch of jungle brush. The thick foliage slowed our descent enough to retain structural integrity. We smashed into the ground and skidded to a stop, shedding little more than glass and paneling.

"I saw Migg moments later when he rushed back to the holding bay. He had a pair of deep gashes across his face, not that you could tell atop his garnet skin. I was slumped against the panels behind the gunner station, battered and bloody, but still alive. We met eyes and he smiled. It should be noted that Durflocks never smile. Ever. They are a calm and dispassionate species with stony demeanors that make them highly effective soldiers and poker players. But Migg smiled that day, and I returned that smile. It was the most impactful moment of my life. I knew, right then and there, that our bond was sacred and unbreakable.

"We stumbled out from the flaming wreckage and into the dense jungle. The ship exploded soon after, vomiting a plume of blazing guts. The shockwave yanked us from our feet and tossed our bodies into the dirt. Our gazes lifted to the sky where the carnage continued to rain. Shuttles rose and departed in constant waves. Most of them made their rendezvous. Many didn't. We learned later that the rookie pilot survived to make 14 troop runs. He even climbed the fleet ranks to become a revered admiral. Migg never took credit, content to own his part in silence. He never spoke of his heroic sacrifice that day, a singular and selfless bravery that I feel privileged to have witnessed. But that's not how they view the world. He had fulfilled his duty and that was enough.

"We gathered our bearings and crept through the thick foliage, hunting for Larrokos. Seeing them on training feeds was one thing, but seeing them face to face was something wholly different. These creatures wore darkness like cloaks of affliction. Their plated bodies were black and burnished, like shards of obsidian crushed into living monsters. Boney ridges protruded from their flesh, creating a natural armor. White eyes, fanged teeth, and razor-sharp claws completed the image of a walking nightmare.

"The first one we encountered took eight plasma blasts to the chest before it fell. At that moment, we realized that our weapons would expend long before the battle ended. We accepted death. Our ends would be met on Kyvon Rai, the great campaign of our time. Whether or not our species survived was out of our hands. Our mission morphed from the whole to the few. We would stare into the eyes of every Larroko we found and remove their stench from the world, or die trying.

"And then the bombs hit.

"We were unaware that our commanders had reached the same conclusion. We had the raw firepower, but not the sustained munitions. After a grim debate, a nuclear option was approved. The cruisers in orbit launched warheads to all primary targets, knowing that countless soldiers would perish in the assault. I cannot imagine a greater weight on my conscience, having to witness annihilation from launch tubes I had opened. Many of those commanders took their own lives after the war.

"The blast reached our eyes well before the shockwave, forcing us to recoil and shield our bodies. Migg and I were fortunate, as the nearest target was inside a mountain pass off in the distance. The impact ripped the bark off trees and tossed us into a jungle stream. A wall of fire raced overhead as we sank into the depths. I gazed up to a rippling surface painted with an orange sheen.

"Migg drowned beneath the waves before I could make sense of it all. The blast had knocked him unconscious and he was floating amid the debris. I cradled him to my chest and swam for shore. As I clawed up the muddy bank, my eyes refused to accept the horrid reality presented to them. The entire world was on fire. Flames danced through the jungle canopy. Embers fell from a scorched sky. Ash curled through the choking air like windswept snow. But I didn't care. Migg needed me and I needed him. I gazed into the shadowy eyes of death and made him a deal. On that day, he would take us both or take his leave. I thumped Migg's chest and breathed life back into his lungs. When he finally revived, he gazed deep into my eyes like a frightened infant. He knew what had transpired. The agony of losing so many brethren paled in comparison to losing each other. He wore that horror, and I mirrored it back to him.

"Much to everyone's surprise, the nuclear assault had granted a reprieve. The Larroko forces fled underground to protect their queen, allowing our own forces to regroup. Up to that point, our ground losses pushed 70%. The reality of the situation became apparent to a fault. If we were to win, we needed to follow the enemy underground.

"And so, we did.

"Migg and I were unaware of that plan. The crash had separated us from the platoons. We had no com device. Our weapons were nearly drained. The skies were burning and we had no bearings. But, we had each other, for however long that would last.

"We settled beneath the smoldering husk of a rompum tree and watched the mushroom cloud rise in the distance. The glowing column and swirling crest served to highlight just how small we were in the great battle of our time. Our races had banded together to fight a fearsome enemy. And fought them we did, inside the grandest of arenas. That war continued to rage, oblivious to our contribution. Migg and I cradled each other and welcomed the end of all things.

"We made love under that rompum tree, consummating a devout friendship built on trust and admiration. It was as challenging as it was beautiful. What Migg lacked in girth, he made up for with talented hands and athletic endurance. I entered his forbidden valley and he explored my caverns, for hours on end. He accepted my savory gifts and returned the kindness innumerable times. We gave in to our greatest desires that night, safe inside each other under the mangled branches of destruction.

"Beneath us, the war raged on.

"We awoke that next morning to the distant howls of elation, like the dull roars of a stadium crowd. Migg and I limped out into a clearing where shuttles were scanning for survivors. We were rescued soon after and learned of the improbable yet hard-fought victory.

"The commanders had detected the queen's location on the opposite side of the moon. After the Larrokos retreated, biosignatures uncovered a large concentration of warriors stationed at the base of a mountain range. The conclusion was made that they were guarding their queen. As a final effort to snuff out the Larroko plague once and for all, the commanders deployed a large team of assassin units to the mountain range. They invaded the cave system and fought through wave after wave of resistance. Most failed, but one succeeded. An elite unit managed to survive the plunge and infiltrate the queen's lair. As they battled the final wave, a Boobybork named Doon sliced through a nest of defenders and plunged his blade into the queen's skull, killing her and the entire Larroko army. Their black bodies fell to the dirt, never to rise again.

"The war had ended.

"The losses were many, but our species had been saved. We returned to our homeworlds under a lasting banner of peace and prosperity. Never again would we fight among each other. We would stand united as a guardian force, one that protects our shared worlds from any and all invaders. And to this day, that pact remains.

"Migg and I parted after the war. Not out of want, but out of necessity. His skills were best served to help rebuild the Durflock fleet. As for me, my place was with my own. The war had left my planet in shambles. My people were destitute and I had an obligation to help those most in need. Migg and I never forgot each other and we kept in contact the best we could. But as with all things in life, your chosen paths take you in different directions. We are not the same creatures we were before, but we remain brothers, and we will always have Kyvon Rai."

A weighted silence fell upon the group.

"Wow," Perra said with a somber tone.

"I know, right?" Max said. "That's his *actual* voice."

Zoey snorted.

"Seriously, I thought he was doing a bit. The guy sounds like an anime princess with an asthma problem."

"Dude!" Perra said, adding a WTF arm spread.

"What? It's like listening to someone pinch the air out of a balloon."

Zoey bit her lips to hold in the laughter.

Henry maintained his longing stare out the viewport.

"C'mon, you have to admit, he sounds like a scholastic toddler."

Zoey burst into laughter.

Perra dropped her jaw and eyed poor Henry as if trying to apologize with her own palpable embarrassment.

The ruckus roused Ross from his nap. He yawned and smacked his lips. "Yo, what'd I miss?"

"Your friends being assholes," Henry said.

"Ha! You sound like a frightened chipmunk."

Zoey howled with laughter.

CHAPTER 13

The freighter ignited hull thrusters as it passed through the transparent barrier of Nifan's stealth ship. A gentle thump brought it to a rest inside the service bay. A flurry of activity surrounded the ship as Boobyborks, Durflocks, and several other curious races prepped for something important. Or at least, something that required a lot of fussing about.

Perra shifted her lips as she studied the bay through the viewport. She eyed a purple-suited humanoid as it scurried around the ship with an armful of hoses. "Hmm," she said, breaking a nervous silence.

Without a word, Henry unlatched his bulky frame and squeezed down the narrow passage to prep Lord Essien for delivery. Ross leapt down from Max's lap and followed the brute. Max, having held back a burning need to pee, sprung to her feet and disappeared into the guest cabin. Zoey and Perra powered down the vessel and unbuckled themselves from the pilot seats. Perra glanced down the passage, then turned a wary gaze to Zoey.

"Given that we fulfilled our end of the agreement, what do you think are the chances that Nifan will let us go on our merry way?"

"Depends. Nifan is many things, but a ransomer she is not."

"Depends on what?"

"Our value. She views us as a commodity, not a threat. Even if we report all of this, nothing will come of it. Hell, I bet the Council of Loken would laugh in our faces. She is already wanted pretty much everywhere. Adding a twig to the log pile won't matter in the slightest."

"So she just keeps us as errand bitches?"

"Possibly, but I doubt it. Remember that we are prized couriers of the PCDS. Nifan traffics intel and they're a large supplier. Ruffling the feathers of bureaucratic governments is one thing, but pissing off a powerful conglomerate would be straight up stupid."

"Quite right," the disembodied voice of Nifan said from behind.

They whipped startled gazes to an empty passage.

Moments later, the hologram image of Nifan assembled inside the cockpit, clad in her silken robes. A matching scarf around her head and neck accented her cobalt eyes. "Hello, ladies."

Perra gawked at the image. "Holographic projection *and* incorporeal presence? I could start religions with that level of technology."

Nifan smirked. "You did well, my lovelies. And Zoey is right. Once Lord Essien is in my custody, you may consider our arrangement fulfilled."

"Arrangement?" Zoey said with a mocking tone. "That's a polite way of saying 'forced undertaking under the threat of death.'"

Perra eyed Zoey with a silent *helping or hurting, dear?*

Nifan narrowed her eyes. "Do not mistake my amenity for gratitude. Your little escapade at Hollow Hold placed you in my debt. You are repaying that debt, be it forced or voluntary. Call it what you wish, but that is how it works out here in the abyss."

Zoey softened her disdain.

"And so, if you are finished waving your dick around, follow me." Nifan turned and sauntered down the narrow passage.

Max emerged from the guest cabin while buckling her pants. "Having to squat every time would definitely prod my patience. That's the first time I have missed my dangle since—" She flinched and froze at the sight of Nifan, now standing face to face.

Nifan gave her a once over and resumed her stride. She floated through Max with the ghostly equivalent of ignoring a homeless person.

Zoey, Perra, and Max slipped through the corridor and into the cargo bay where Henry had detached Lord Essien from the pipe. He re-cuffed her hands in front like a proper prisoner. Ross watched from a crate stack before losing any and all interest. He yawned and started grooming his chest with a ridiculous neck-down stroke. Nifan moseyed over to Essien and faced her like a steely drill sergeant. Henry stood tall beside the captive, maintaining a firm grip on her upper arm. Nifan glanced at the brute and offered a slight nod. He pinched the bag on Essien's head and yanked it free.

Essien's miffed expression morphed into pure disdain at the sight of her nemesis. She reared back and spat at Nifan. The lugie sailed through Nifan's cheek and struck the crate where Ross sat. He poofed with fright, then glared around the group before returning to his tongue bath. Essien heaved with rage, popping the leather across her chest.

"Kidnapping is a coward's weapon."

"Kidnapping implies a ransom, dear. My intentions are far more specific."

"With all due respect, I would rather be skinned alive by the Dread Jacks."

"Your respect is not required."

Lord Essien walked her gaze up a meaty arm to Henry, who glared back at her through a stony face. She grimaced and glanced around the cargo bay before returning her eyes to Nifan. "Get on with it, then."

"Get on with what?"

Essien narrowed her gaze. "Don't play games with me, faux posh. Snatching me off Jarovy takes steel-plated balls. You need me badly for something, so get on with it."

Nifan replied with a half-grin, then nodded at Henry.

The brute re-bagged Lord Essien and jerked her towards the airlock. He thumped the wall panel, opening the door to a bustling service bay. After a quick scan, he grabbed Essien by the waist and flung her over a shoulder, drawing a yelp and curse. He dropped to the ground with a heavy thud and started tromping towards the service doors on the far wall, paying no mind to the crew.

"Follow him to my chambers," Nifan said to the group, then crackled away.

Zoey sighed and turned to Perra, who mirrored a glum expression. They gathered Max and Ross and led them out of the vessel, dropping one by one to a polished floor. The airlock slid closed, leaving them to the roar of a swarming bay. Rusted shuttles arrived and departed with the aid of a meticulous choreography. The green energy barrier pulsed with each puncture, a goading reminder that a thin curtain protected everyone from the vacuum of space.

Max studied the familiar shuttles and recognized them as the same fleet from the Grondon outpost. She grunted to herself and eyed the hover droids overhead as they hauled tools and supplies to the hands that needed them.

Migg's Ripper sat parked on a nearby platform with its tendrils in stirrups. A team of Durflocks hustled around the ship, tending to repairs and giving it a much-needed shine. Migg stood beside it with a clipboard in hand, checking off a lengthy to-do list. His big yellow eyes followed Henry as he passed. They gave each other firm salutes.

The sexual tension was palpable.

The group squeezed into an elevator car and enjoyed a tense yet uneventful ride up to Nifan's condo. Henry filled most of one side with Lord Essien draped over his shoulder. Zoey, Perra, and Max filled the other side with Ross seated at the center. Everyone stared at the doors in silence as the elevator climbed to the top floor. A pleasant melody served as a backdrop to the collective discomfort. Essien squirmed atop Henry's beefy frame, then grunted with frustration.

"Could someone, um, scratch my backside?"

Silence responded.

Perra cleared her throat.

"Fine, fuck all of you then."

Max, feeling a tug of sympathy, reached up and cupped Essien's leather-clad buttocks. "Here?"

"Lower."

Max slid her hand down. "Here?"

"Closer to the crack."

"Here?"

"Yes, yes, that's the spot."

Max dug her fingernails into the soft leather, drawing a moan from Essien.

Zoey shook her head.

Perra closed her eyes and imagined herself anywhere but there.

"Okay, that's enough," Essien said.

Max removed her hand and resumed a forward stare.

Essien shivered with relief and paused before forcing a pair of vile words from her throat. "Thank you."

"Welcome."

"I will take that kindness into consideration once I free myself and murder you all."

"Uh ... thanks."

The elevator dinged and the doors slid open, revealing Nifan's opulent abode. Henry tromped onto the floor pelts with little regard for decorum. He dropped Lord Essien into a waiting chair, then clasped his hands behind his back and stood guard over her shoulder. The energy shackles around her wrists hummed and crackled, needling the dead air.

The rest of the crew crept inside and settled around the lime green couch. Max leaned back into the plush cushions and expelled a sigh of contentment. She glanced around the pad and nodded like a redneck in a lavish castle. Platters of refreshments adorned the table, creating an inviting spread that pleased the eye as much as the stomach. Zoey studied the morsels with a skeptical glare as Max proceeded to stuff her mouth with reckless abandon. Perra, satisfied with the unintentional poison test, plucked a handful of noms from the heap to quiet a rumbling stomach. Zoey grimaced, then followed her lead.

"I treat my guests very well," Nifan said as she floated out from a nearby nook. A fresh martini swirled between her fingers, garnished with olives and a splash of ostentation. A silken train flowed behind her, showcasing a pleasant blend of greens and blues. The fabric draped across her chest and up over her shoulders, leaving her head and neck exposed. Various rings and a simple necklace completed the swanky ensemble. Her ashen skin seemed smooth and vital, almost innocent. Prominent cheekbones painted shadows beneath her eyes. Locks of white hair twisted into a lavish hairstyle befit for royalty. The Dossier, embodiment of mystery, had preened for this occasion.

"These are incredible," Max said through a mouthful of munchies. She forced a large swallow down her throat and licked her fingers afterwards.

"And expensive," Nifan said. "Few can afford Yucaran penises these days."

Max had the next noodle inside her mouth when the info smacked her brain. A horrified pause turned into a reluctant chew and finished with a strained swallow. She studied the plate of phallic snacks while chewing on her lip.

"That's new," Ross said. "They're usually attached to something when she puts them in her mouth."

Zoey and Perra snort-laughed.

Henry cracked a rare smile.

Nifan grinned as she sauntered over to the chair across from Lord Essien. The seats were arranged in an interview setting, complete with a small table for Nifan's ever-present cocktail. Waves of thin fabric slithered across the opposing chair as Nifan lowered into the cushions. Her eyes crawled over her adversary, studying her breaths and posture. She savored every tense moment. With a final sip, she lowered the glass onto the table and nodded at Henry, who pinched the bag and yanked it free.

Lord Essien recoiled at the rush of light. Her squinting eyes surveyed the immediate area before landing on Nifan. Teeth gnashed as she reared back and spat again, but this time into Henry's hand as he snapped it between them. He used the wet palm to smack her across the cheek, silencing the snarls with her own spittle. She lobbed a glare over her shoulder and returned to a smirking Nifan.

Zoey and Perra watched from the nearby couch, riveted by the unfolding drama. Max continued to munch away on the penile treats while Ross snickered between each one.

"You look well," Nifan said.

"Says the smirking whore who destroyed my fleet."

"Well, considering your—"

"You tried to fucking murder me. Pardon my insolence, but we are well beyond pleasantries. What the fuck do you want?"

"We didn't used to be."

"Be what?"

"Beyond pleasantries."

Essien leaned forward, causing Henry to stiffen.

Nifan waved him off with a subtle gesture.

"The last time I checked," Essien said, "it was *you* who disappeared."

Nifan grinned, but this time through a fog of guilt. "You knew very well that I had to—"

"Had to what? Build an empire based on bullshit? You leveraged a juicy piece of intel to become a glorified leaker. That's all you are. You flushed our entire relationship down the toilet to become a weaponized gasbag."

"Awwww snap!" Ross said.

Everyone turned to the kitty on the couch, now wearing a cheeky smile.

Ross shrugged. "What? Big reveal, just playing my part as the audience. This shit is better than Springer."

"Are you kidding?" Max said. "Springer was trash TV at its finest. This is more like, um, Dr. Phil or something. There was this one time when a nudist couple wanted to adopt a donkey and—"

"Dude, uncool. You're being rude."

"Huh?"

"Another show is already in progress."

Max glanced around the group, only to realize that all eyes were hate-locked on her like a movie talker. "Ah, now I'm the asshole. That is some ninja-like buck-passing."

Zoey cleared her throat.

"Forgive my ill-mannered associate," Ross said. "Please continue."

Nifan raked a stink eye over the audience and returned her attention to an irate Lord Essien. She studied her former lover with a mix of sympathy and restraint. A delicate hand plucked the martini from the side table. She took a light sip and shifted in her seat. "And what about you?"

Essien shrugged. "What about me?"

"You funneled your rage into one of the most nefarious criminal factions the universe has ever seen."

"It seems we have both enjoyed success."

"Success?" Nifan chuckled. "You ran riot over any fleet, family, or faction you pleased. If sheer brutality is your unit of measurement, then yes, you have been quite successful."

"And how many innocent beings have lost their lives to your crooked affairs? Not to point out the obvious, but the consequences of shady dealings are the dealer's to bear."

Nifan smiled. "Always a clever girl."

"Clever bitch, you mean."

The tone softened a bit.

"I have a gift for you."

Essien huffed. "And what could you possibly offer that I would actually want?"

Nifan tossed back a final sip, stood from her plush seat, and strolled towards the rear bar. "Rojan pyek."

The shackles around Lord Essien's wrists crackled and vanished. A sudden tension ensnared the chamber. Essien opened and closed her freed hands, as if to inspect a shiny new weapon. With a slow and steady pace, she gripped the armrests and climbed to her feet. Her purple skull twisted above a taut bust as silver eyes scanned the room. Black lips remained puckered and primed for combat. She eyed each mortal before settling on Henry. His sunken eyes and rigid frame responded loud and clear with *try anything and I'll rip your head from your body.*

"Come, join me," Nifan said.

Essien took a weighted breath and stepped towards the rear wall with Henry in tow. Nifan plucked another martini glass from a near-by tray and started shaking a drink mixer. She refilled her own glass and poured another. A skewer of olives dropped into each beverage as Essien took her final steps. Henry veered off to the side and resumed a guarded position. Nifan lifted the glass from the counter and offered it to her esteemed guest. Essien accepted it with a wary hand and glared at Nifan without taking a sip.

"Relax," Nifan said. "Poison is a boring dispatch."

"So is blackmail."

Nifan grinned and offered a gentle toast before taking a healthy swig.

Essien sighed and returned the gesture, then took a wary sip while maintaining eye contact.

Nifan bit her lower lip and awaited a response.

The group held their collective breath.

After a long and restive silence, Essien smacked her lips and moaned with delight. "Goddamn, you do make a great martini."

"Qarakish gin with zorium mist, none of that vermouth crap."

"You never were a fan of Earth."

"Still not, irrespective of Maxine's notable talents." She glanced at Max and winked.

Max scrunched her brow.

"You don't want to know," Ross said to Max.

Nifan turned to the rear wall. "Gracomas."

The wall flickered and faded into an expansive view of the Terramesh. Jaws slacked open with the reveal, creating an enormous panorama of the bonded worlds. The distant supergiant bathed the cluster with a golden sheen. Sunlight reflected off the mangled web, glimmering in the black like glitter dust. Nifan and Lord Essien studied the mighty mesh while sipping on their expensive cocktails.

"Do you remember our first romantic getaway?"

Essien closed her eyes and nodded. "That delightful bed and breakfast on Xonora."

"That's right. And, we had a lovely conversation over a candlelit dinner. Do you remember it?"

"I will never forget it. That was when we confessed our deepest and darkest desires. It was the first time I told you about my longing for—" Her gaze widened and snapped to Nifan. "You didn't."

Nifan replied with a loving smile. "I did."

Henry stepped forward and placed a jewelry box on the counter, drawing a slack-jawed response from Lord Essien. She stared at the tiny box and covered her mouth with both hands. Her eyes began to water with a rush of elation.

"Go on, open it."

Essien lifted the box with a trembling hand. She expelled a fluttering breath and flipped the lid, revealing a shiny red button attached to a transmitter. "I ... I can't believe you did this for me."

"Call it a long-overdue apology."

Essien locked eyes with her former lover.

Nifan nodded. "Go ahead, you deserve it."

Essien smiled and turned a tearful gaze to the mesh. Her thumb traced the edge of the red button as she drank in the magnificent vista. A warm blanket of peace and contentment cradled her being, ridding her mind of fury.

She pushed the button.

CHAPTER 14

Back on Grondon, Jai sat upon a small boulder deep inside a cliff cavern. Limp hands hung from dirty knees, soaking up warmth from a small campfire. A flickering flame reflected off tired eyes. Cracked lips emerged from a layer of frozen saliva, giving his mouth a much-needed soak. He stared at the opposite wall several meters away, a blank canvas of blackened stone that allowed his mind to reset.

Jai and his Trevor cloak had followed the river basin and discovered an ancient lava chute. He gathered an armful of twigs and brush, then ventured down into the cave until he could feel his face again. The craggy tunnel offered a warm reprieve from the unforgiving landscape. The local wildlife used the tunnel for the exact same reason, as evidenced by the putrid air and fresh droppings. Jai had pressed on until he stubbed his toe on a small boulder. A stumble, yelp, and sigh concluded his exploration. He dropped the brush, set it aflame, and cursed the need to do so.

Despite the predicament, Jai enjoyed a rare moment of peace and quiet. The roaring wind faded to a distant hum. For once, he could hear his own breath and sense his heart beating inside his chest. Neck bones popped as he rolled his head from side to side, prompting a moan and scowl. His gaze fell to a blood-stained blazer that raised and lowered with each breath. The corner of his comdev poked through the fabric, hooking his attention. He reached into his breast pocket and retrieved the device. The screen was shattered, likely from the crash or the freezing water, maybe both. He grunted and tossed it into the floor muck.

A steady drip of blood echoed around the hollow, even though Jai was unharmed. Green drops spurted from his fashionable Trevor cloak. They splashed into the muck, only to slither back into the gutted body and fall again. Chunks of flesh had followed Jai into the cavern, desperate to reunite with their owner. Trevor's lifeless head flopped backwards like a sweater hood. Flimsy arms draped across Jai's chest with hands bound at the wrists. A bloody torso sliced from groin to neck clung to Jai's back like a grisly cape.

Having restored some circulation, Jai removed his gory cloak and tossed it over the fire. It splatted against a rock on the other side, like a wet towel hitting a tile floor. Flesh nubs and green puddles rushed over to merge with the pile. Soon after, a reconstituted Trevor began to stir. An array of wet snaps filled the cavern, like a rookie doctor resetting a bone over and over. With a final clack, Trevor blinked to life and started to assess the situation. The crackling embers hooked his attention first. He eyed the broken comdev, then raked his gaze over the interior. It took a little while, but he finally locked eyes with the meaty thug staring at him through the flames. Trevor flinch-yelped, then grumbled and crossed his arms like a petulant child.

"That was a dick move," he said.

Jai raised an eyebrow.

"We could have cuddled to achieve the same effect."

Jai lowered the eyebrow.

"But, but, I can see why you did it. Just, warn me next time." Trevor grimaced as he stretched away some gutting soreness. "So where are we?"

"In a cave."

"Duh."

Jai tightened his gaze.

Trevor immediately tempered his attitude. "No, sorry, I mean, are we still on Grondon or what?"

"Yeah, a few klicks up from the crash. But, we have no coms, no food, no nothing. We need a workable plan to get off this rock."

"On it." Trevor crossed his legs, folded his hands, and closed his eyes, assuming a contemplation pose.

Jai shook his head.

Trevor thought for a while, then grasped his knees and opened his eyes. "Any chance the ship coms survived?"

"The ship was on fire before it sank into an icy river."

"So, no chance?"

"Feel free to swim out and check."

Trevor sneered in response.

Jai rubbed his face and exhaled a heavy sigh. "Our best bet is to hike back to the rebel outpost. Maybe they deserted in haste, left some ports unlocked. If we're lucky, we might be able to—" Jai froze for a moment, then raised a puzzled gaze to the ceiling.

"What? What's wrong?"

"Did you hear that?"

Trevor shrugged. "Hear what?"

Jai grabbed a burning branch from the fire and climbed to his feet. He held the torch overhead and started walking towards the entrance. Trevor stood from the dirty floor and followed close behind as Jai hurried down the tunnel with a laser-like focus. The peculiar thumps, like bass drums off in the distance, grew louder and louder as they neared the exit. Jai rounded a final corner, bringing the white landscape of Grondon into view. He stepped outside onto the cliff ledge and surveyed the river basin. Nothing. The rumbling rapids served as a muted backdrop. Puffs of steam rose from the torch as snow flurries needled the flame.

Another boom, this time distinctly overhead.

Jai clenched his lips and lifted his gaze to the sky.

Trevor unleashed a blood-curdling shriek and staggered backwards. He tripped over a rock, tumbled to the ground, scrambled to his feet, and disappeared into the cave.

Jai continued his perplexing study of the sky, wondering when his brain would stop fucking with him. The ground rumbled beneath his feet, spilling snow over the ledge and confirming the batshit crazy insanity infecting his eye holes. He nodded, spun around, and sprinted back into the cave while screaming like a banshee.

The image of shattered planetary pillars filled the skies of Grondon (and every other world inside the Terramesh). Gigantic shards of steel shimmered overhead, the remnants of massive nuclear blasts. The sky bridges had peeled back like mangled flowers, freeing the worlds from bondage. A lethal rain of shrapnel tore through the space in between, destroying ships and painting atmospheres with streaks of fire. The unbound planets began to roam inside a cauldron of gravitational chaos.

A monstrous shockwave hit the planet surface, jostling the cavern and ripping cracks along the interior. Slabs of rock detached from the ceiling and splashed into the muck. Trevor shuffled his screams and curses as he trotted down the tunnel. Jai caught up and slammed Trevor into the wall as he passed. Another shockwave hit the surface. Fissures swelled, dropping giant boulders into the cavern. Jai kept a frantic pace with torch outstretched, wearing an expression of terrified determination. The guiding flame faded into the distance as Trevor lagged behind.

Jai skidded to a halt inside a large opening. His meager torch failed to illuminate the whole interior. Frightened eyes scanned the darkness for a glimmer of hope. Trevor caught up soon after, opting to hang back at the cavern mouth. Jai spun around in the dark empty, his hurried breaths turning into grunts of panic.

A deafening crash shook the hollow, triggering a violent earthquake. The impact tossed them to the ground. A fissure split the opening down the center, revealing a lake of boiling lava far below. A fiery glow filled the crevasse as sections of the floor crumbled and fell away. Jai scurried back from the chasm and pinned himself against the wall. He glanced over to Trevor, who clung to the cave mouth for dear life. Stone and dust continued to rain into the tunnel. Another violent crash ripped chunks of rock from the walls and ceiling. Jai waved Trevor over, only to watch a boulder fall and crush him. A splatter of blood and guts painted the floor green.

Jai recoiled, then shrugged. "He'll be fine."

He continued down the perilous ledge, crawling on all fours towards another cave. The lava below started to rise, prompting Jai to yelp and scurry forward like a frightened toddler. A thunderous crack pierced his ears as a section of the floor ahead broke off and fell away. It splashed into the lava below, tossing ribbons of molten rock onto the walls. Jai barked with frustration and whipped his gaze around for another out. Nothing. With death closing in, he was forced to climb to the next ledge. He grabbed a solid hold along the jagged wall and lifted his meaty frame. At that moment, the ledge beneath him gave way and fell into the fire, leaving him to the mercy of his own grip.

Jai Ferenhal dangled above a lake of lava with nothing but his finger strength preventing death. He glanced at the tunnel, then down to the lava, then back to the tunnel, then over to the splatter that used to be Trevor. With his fate all but determined, he closed his eyes and banged his forehead against the rock, barking curses with each hit.

And now he saw stars. Or rather, what he thought were stars. Ribbons of light started swirling around his dangling body. His fingers trembled as the glowing cocoon built to a crescendo. He closed his eyes and gnashed his teeth, but the last of his strength left his body. Wails of despair escaped his lungs as he started to fall, but a blinding flash yanked him into the ether.

* * *

Lord Essien squealed with delight as the 86 unshackled planets of the Terramesh crashed into each other. The shiny red button had triggered a monumental fireworks display, compliments of cleaver nukes placed along the pylons. The blasts severed the mighty pillars like razors through string. Their signature red discs expanded from white-hot bursts, freeing every world from bondage and gifting them to the gods of gravity. The planets swirled like marbles in a bowl before succumbing to a colossal crunch. The city planet of Jarovy dis-appeared beneath an onslaught of falling sky. 86 worlds fused into a single lumpy mass. The impacts threw giant chunks of earth into or-bit, resembling a haze of dust. The red rings of annihilation faded into nothing, leaving a calamity of unspeakable proportions.

Nifan floated over to her mistress and cradled her arm while gauging her reaction. Essien remained enchanted by the grisly sight, sporting a wide grin that exposed her teeth. She squeezed Nifan's hand and sniffled.

"This is the most beautiful thing I have ever seen," she said, then met eyes with Nifan. "Thank you."

"My gift to you," Nifan said.

They leaned in for a kiss.

Zoey, Perra, and Max stood off to the side, donning an array of horrified faces. Zoey cupped the back of her head and contorted her mouth like a baby eating broccoli. Perra covered her face with both hands and peeked through her fingers, as if hate-watching a snuff film. Max spanned the spectrum, shifting between utter confusion and dry heaves. Even Henry raised his eyebrows, the Boobybork equivalent of a terrified gasp. Ross, on the other hand, responded with a nod of admiration and remained on the couch for a crotch licking session. After all, the Fifth Force of Nature had seen (and caused) some serious shit.

"And just like that," Nifan said to Essien, "you are the sole sur-vivor of your race, just like me."

"I haven't the words," Essien said. "It's more beautiful than I could have ever imagined."

"Like you."

Essien giggled and cradled her lover's arm.

"Let me get this straight," Perra said as she lowered her hands to her chest. "You planned this entire thing ... to win back your girl-friend?"

Nifan smirked. "We do anything for the ones we love."

Perra twitched an eye. "*What?*"

Zoey clawed at her lips and cheeks. "You just murdered countless civilizations to impress an ex? Fuck me sideways, what's wrong with flowers?"

Essien shrugged. "Genocide is kinda my thing."

"I know my Essy Wessy," Nifan said.

The ladies giggled and kissed again.

"That ..." Max said, searching for the proper phrase to convey her shock and awe, "... is hardcore."

"You guys are easily impressed," Ross said.

The group turned to the feline on the couch.

"Just saying, I've seen grander tokens of affection."

Nifan grunted and crossed her arms. "Like what?"

"Ever heard of the Sheevian Titans?"

Blank stares responded.

Ross grimaced and shook his head. "No, of course you haven't. They were godlike beings that once roamed the far reaches of the universe. When they copulated, they triggered radioactive discharges that made gamma-ray bursts look like firecrackers. Their lustful thrusting created enough force and energy to forge new elements. There's a better than average chance that the metal around your neck was created during one of their star-destroying orgasms. Their courtship dances disrupted the flows of galaxies, causing gravitational waves that warped the very fabric of spacetime."

Essien deflated a bit.

Nifan glared at the feline.

"But no, this was cute." Ross shrug-nodded and offered a furry thumbs-up. "Good job."

Nifan stepped to the couch and leaned over it, resting her fists on the cushions. "Cute? *Cute?* This was a brilliant fucking piece of intricate planning, you little shit. This was an opera of chaos, a symphony of destruction. Every felled city, every snuffed civilization, every death, all of it, for the woman I love. I wrought—"

Ross yawned. "Sorry, keep going."

Nifan huffed in a rare moment of fluster.

Essien rushed over to intervene. She hooked Nifan's arm and pulled her from the couch while rubbing her back like a comforting mother. "It's okay, just ignore him. The gift was perfect. I loved it, truly and honestly."

Nifan lowered her voice. "Little prick thinks he knows true love."

"I know, he thinks he knows everything."

Ross winked at Nifan.

"Dude," Max said to Ross, then spread her arms as if to shout *why the fuck are you goading a criminal mastermind that just joined the mass-murdering hall of fame?*

Ross smirked and tilted his head, replying with *like, duh, ye forget who I am?*

Max slouched and grimaced.

"Question," Zoey said with a touch of bother. "Am I the only one here still tripping biscuits over 86 planets worth of cold-blooded carnage?"

Perra raised her hand.

Nifan jerked free from Essien's grasp and stomped over to Zoey. Her malicious gaze burned into the Mulgawat as a final step brought them face to face. "Carnage? No, this is creation. I have given birth to a new empire."

Zoey shook her head. "Only a coward kills from afar."

Nifan slapped her across the cheek, whipping her head to the side. Zoey returned her gaze with a slow twist, eyeing her adversary through a spiteful glare. Perra stepped behind her beau and grasped her shoulder.

"Mind your tongue, Mulgawat. You retain your head by my grace alone."

"You said our obligation was fulfilled," Perra said from over Zoey's shoulder. "I think it's time for us to go."

Nifan let out a sinister chuckle. "Silly girl, you think this is over? Oh no, little lamb. Your role in this revival has just begun."

Zoey wiped a dollop of blood from her lip. "I'm not sure I heard you correctly."

"Yes you did."

"You want to roll those dice with the Council of Loken? Or the

PCDS?"

Nifan glanced into the black where the Terramesh husk floated like a mangled corpse. "What makes you think I fear a bunch of peacekeepers or a courier company?"

Zoey stowed her breath.

Nifan locked eyes with her. "On this day, I render their power and influence obsolete. I do not fear them, nor do I contend with them. I *am* them."

Zoey glanced back to Perra, who reflected the dejection. A heavy sigh escaped her lungs as she surveyed the field of destruction. She bowed her head for a moment, then donned a submissive gaze.

"Good girl," Nifan said with a soft whisper and stroked her cheek with the back of her hand.

Zoey squirmed and recoiled.

"Your role from here is actually quite simple. Remember what you saw today and proclaim it to the universe. I want every Loken member, every courier, and every drunkard in every port to know that a new era has begun. You tell them all that The Dossier and Lord Essien have united to rule the black. Our reign shall—"

A violent crash jostled the stealth ship, yanking everyone off their feet. Nifan and Essien tumbled backwards into the bar and kissed the floor. Snifters shot from the counter and smashed to pieces. Henry pinned himself against a wall and drew his pistol. Zoey and Perra staggered into the nearby couch and tumbled over the side. Ross sank his claws into the cushions, ripping the expensive fabric. The coffee table hurled into the wall and shattered on impact, raining penis treats and other noms around the room. Max thumped her back to the floor, forcing the air from her lungs. She hooked an arm around a bar leg and gasped for breath.

Lord Essien scrambled to her feet and whipped her gaze around the chamber. "The fuck was that?!"

Another blast rattled the ship and sent her tumbling to the floor.

"Tatia, report!" Nifan said.

"Unknown assailants," the stealth ship AI said. "Shields ineffective."

"What?! That's impossible!"

"What tech are you using?" Essien said.

"Halim design, above high-military. It's impenetrable."

"Apparently not."

Another blast rumbled the ship, prompting a barrage of yelps and curses. Nifan clung to a bar leg as glasses smashed the floor around her. Zoey and Perra fought for balance atop a wandering sofa. Ross remained affixed to the cushion and rode it like a plush surfboard. Lord Essien pressed her palms to the transparent wall and tried to assess the situation. Her gaze darted around the black before spotting a curious sight above the ship.

"What the fuck are those things?"

Max angled for a view, then burst into laughter.

"What is it?" Zoey said.

Max slowed to a giggle and turned to Nifan. "Oh wow, you done pissed off the nerd brigade."

CHAPTER 15

Seven figures in crimson cloaks sat around a crescent bench inside a dim and empty arena. Spotlights overhead encased them in hazy cones of luminescence. Sagging hoods painted dark shadows across their chests, cloaking identities under an air of secrecy. Arms and tentacles folded across the table surface, resting in wait.

The bench sat upon the first of many seating tiers, giving the ensemble an elevated perspective. At the center of the arena, an additional spotlight dropped a large white circle onto an empty floor. Motes of dust wandered through the harsh light. Nubs and fingertips rapped upon the wooden bench, prodding a restive silence. The middle figure took a weighted breath and exhaled a fluttering sigh. The largest of the group reached into his lap and plucked a cracker from a hidden bag. The resulting crunches nabbed the attention of his cohorts, who huffed and shook their heads.

A crackle of static echoed from the center, followed by a flicker of light. It swirled into a glowing ribbon, building up speed and forming a cocoon. A winding hum filled the room and peaked with a pop of electric charge. The cocoon spat out a screaming Jai Ferenhal into the central spotlight. His body thumped the floor with a harsh thud and the ribbons fizzled away. He continued screaming until realizing that the cold metal was not a lake of lava.

Silence returned to the arena.

Jai palmed the metal plane with a mixture of confusion and relief. He rose onto all fours and studied the immediate area, uncovering little more than a well-lit floor in need of a good sweep. With a measured calm and a hint of worry, he climbed to his feet and spun in a slow circle. Specks of dirt fell from his soiled suit and glimmered in the bright light. A final turn uncovered seven mysterious figures sitting behind a large crescent podium. He wiped the sweat from his brow and shielded his eyes for a better look.

"Jai Ferenhal," said the central figure in a mousy voice.

"Y—yes?"

"Cruvion race of the Parlech Quadrant, comrade of the Veiled Traders, disgraced member of the PCDS, and trusted confidant of a one Lord Essien."

"Um, sure."

"Do you know where you are?"

Jai glanced around the ominous chamber, then back to the panel. "Purgatory?"

"You're not dead."

"Night club?"

"There's no music."

"Suth'ra Station, final answer."

"Goddamnit!" Jerry said, then flipped his hood over his shoulders. "Did I not say that snatching the human was a bad idea? It completely killed our mythos."

"Does it really matter at this point?" Yerba said.

"Yes," Gorp said in his gruff amphibious voice. "I have to agree with Jerry. Anonymity is our most precious asset."

Kaeli cleared her throat. "I thought intelligence was our most precious asset."

"And coffee," Frank said.

Carl facepalmed himself.

Jai shifted his puckered lips.

"I think we can all agree," Yerba said, "that intelligence is our top asset, followed by anonymity, and then coffee."

"Disagree," Gorp said. "Anonymity is paramount, which allows us the capacity for intellectual dominance. Coffee is a distant third."

"Third?" Frank said. "I would argue that without decent coffee, this whole charade would be in the shitter. Have you ever done quantum calculus without a pot of mud?"

"Hmm," Gorp said. "A valid point."

Jerry groused. "What's the point of good coffee without great cloaking tech? I think it's anonymity, then coffee, then intelligence."

Kaeli chuckled. "Are you seriously ranking intelligence third? A halfwit child could drink coffee in secret."

Fio slammed his fists upon the table. "Everyone shut the fuck up!"

A tense silence infected the room.

Fio refolded his hands. "Jai Ferenhal."

Jai ruffled his brow. "Still yes."

"You have been summoned here by the almighty Suth'ra because we have learned of a troubling situation. An unholy alliance between Orantha Nifan and Lord Essien is brewing in the black."

Jai shrugged. "News to me."

"The Suth'ra Society has maintained a neutral presence inside the universe. We are an uncaring eye wandering the cosmos. But alas, our neglect permitted the rise of the war criminal Halim, a former colleague and total wackadoodle. He single-handedly destroyed the entire Varokin fleet at the Battle of Hollow Hold, a massacre you witnessed firsthand alongside Lord Essien. Against all odds, you survived while donning a pink tutu."

Jai grimaced. "Thank you for that."

"The survival of Lord Essien was unlucky, but benign. Her armada was in shambles and her supposed enemy had fled into hiding. However, this budding union between the two cannot happen. It would be like Adolf Hitler colluding with Morgok the World Crusher. The balance of the entire universe would be at risk."

"And what does that have to do with me?"

"You fought beside Lord Essien. She trusted you."

"I wouldn't go that far."

"Regardless, you have acquired intimate knowledge of her tactics and demeanor. Thus, you have become a valuable asset to the resistance."

"Resistance? The Suth'ra are going to war?"

"*Everyone* is going to war. The battle of our age is about to begin. And you, Jai Ferenhal, will play a vital role in the days to come."

Jai thought for a moment. "So I'm a snitch."

"No, no, nooo. You are an esteemed informant, a vessel of intelligence, a fleshy database of triumph. You will guide our mighty forces into the warring war of wars. Your wealth of opposition strategy will raise the iron fist of victory."

Jai rolled his eyes. "So I'm a *really big* snitch."

"No, no, not at all." Fio grunted with frustration, then gestured to the group. "Someone, anyone, a little help."

"Mighty warrior," Jerry said. "You are tasked with—"

"Guys," Jai said with a polite chuckle. "I am so messing with you. Count me in. That raging bitch has done nothing but bust my balls since Europa."

"Oh thank goodness," Fio said, then bowed his head to restore some menace.

"Noble champion," Jerry said. "You shall rest in holding while our forces are mobilized. An initial strike has already commenced."

"Fine by me. Just point me to the showers."

Several chuckles rose from the bench.

"Oh no," Fio said with a cocky snicker. "Not here. Your intellectual inferiority would dick-punch morale and bleach the walls with idiocy."

Jai huff-chuckled. "Wow, you have mastered the subtle art of ingratiation."

The assembly huddled for a brief mumble, then restored their rigid postures.

"That is an incorrect statement," Fio said.

Jai started to respond, but opted for a sigh and facepalm. He groused for a bit, then returned his attention to the panel. "So if not here, then where?"

"Stand by for transport," Yerba said.

Jai recoiled as a static charge sparked to life and swirled around him. A ribbon of light raced in circles, enclosing his meaty frame. The rushing energy climbed to a final jolt and yanked Jai into the ether.

Moments later, he stood at the base of a giant mountain range. With eyes widened and mouth agape, he surveyed a desolate landscape full of rolling hills and craggy boulders. Clouds crept along the towering cliff sides. A sapphire lake shimmered off in the distance. Jai paused to gather his wits and inhaled some of the cleanest air he had ever tasted. His eyelids fell to savor the moment. Lungs swelled with elation until his ears uncovered a silent world. No birds or animals, no ships or stations, just a gentle breeze and an eerie sense of isolation.

Jai released his breath, opened his eyes, and flinched at the sudden appearance of a giant boulder in front of him. He spun around in confusion, but everything seemed in place. Hasty blinks and eye rubs failed to mend the hallucination. He took a cautious step forward and pressed an open palm to the surface. It was warm and leathery, like the skin of an elephant.

Then it quivered.

Jai yelped and jerked backwards.

"New touchie!" Phil said and sprouted a fresh gaggle of tentacles. They wrapped around a horrified Jai and slurped him into the mass.

* * *

A swarm of Suth'ra orbs floated above Nifan's cruiser. Their viewport slivers glowed red, like a congress of *Knight Rider* superfans. Each wore a Mohawk of antennae, as if to perpetuate the salty nature of punk rockers. The ebon hulls of everyone present infected the area with precisely nothing. That is, until an orb sparked with electric charge and shot a bolt of chaos into the cruiser.

The cruiser rattled and rumbled with each strike, like a naive crocodile getting blasted by an electric eel. Tendrils of lightning slithered around the hull before crackling into the black. Inside the bridge, the group clung to their respective balance keepers, be it a bar leg, a sturdy couch, or a helpful section of wall. Art frames and expensive sculptures rested in pieces across the floor. A dignified chamber had morphed into the stylistic merit of a teenager's bedroom.

"I'm just gonna put this out there," Essien said to Nifan. "Your ethics were so compromised by this scheme, that you provoked an intervention by the Suth'ra Society. That is the sexiest thing I have ever seen."

Nifan smirked and bit her lower lip.

"So what's the plan, my love?"

Nifan turned to Henry against the wall. "Rally Migg and summon the armada. I want both fleets to our back as soon as possible."

Henry nodded and jogged towards the elevator.

"Tatia! Damage report!"

"Hull intact," the ship AI said. "No structural damage. All systems online and operational."

"How can that be?" Essien said.

"Protonic blasts. They're not trying to kill us. They just want our attention."

A large panel along the transparent wall crackled with an incoming signal. The group relaxed a bit and climbed to their feet as the hologram bust of Fio pieced itself together above the counter, his face hidden beneath a crimson robe. The mutilated remnants of the Terramesh floated along the wall behind him, creating a lurid backdrop. Nifan, Essien, Zoey, and Perra formed a half-circle around the hologram. Ross detached from a tattered cushion and trotted over to a shattered sculpture. He tossed a nod to Max, who opted out of the unfolding drama and moseyed away from the bar.

Jerry cleared his throat from off-hologram. "Humble thy loins, for you are in the presence of His Impeccable Majesty, Grandmaster Fiolandon, High Lord of the Suth'ra Council, Speaker of Truth, Defender of Reason."

Essien crossed her arms and scowled. "And you are in the presence of Orantha Nifan, The Dossier, Breaker of Balls, Giver of No Fucks."

Fio gasped and shook his fist. "How dare ye disrespect the mighty Suth'ra! Ye shall rue the day that—"

Jerry grabbed Fio's outstretched arm and lowered it to the table. "Calm down, dude."

Fio whipped his gaze off-hologram and shook his fist at Jerry. "How dare ye disrespect thy fearless leader! Ye shall rue the day! Rue it, I say!"

Jerry sighed. "Sweet Sagan on a pogo stick, do you hear yourself right now?"

Fio stammered a bit, then grumbled some curses before resuming his not-so-ominous posture. "Orantha Nifan and Lord Essien. You are to lay down arms and turn yourselves over to the Council of Loken, lest you be erased from existence by the full force of the Suth'ra Society."

Lord Essien puffed her chest for another verbal assault, but Nifan grabbed her arm. Essien clenched her lips shut as Nifan took a step forward. She straightened her ruffled dress and donned a devious smirk. "Master Fio, there are just so many ways to say *no*. I could go with the classic *kiss my ass*, perhaps an exuberant *piss off*. But for this most asinine of requests, I am forced to concoct an appropriate retaliatory response. That said, please accept my humble request to *eat shit and die, you dirty little nerd fuck*."

Fio paused to digest the retort, then slammed his fists on the table. "How dare ye disrespect the mighty Suth'ra!"

"Goddamnit, Fio!" Jerry said, prompting a slap fight.

In the rear of the chamber, Ross trotted around a busted sculpture to an empty cube stand. He gave it a once over, leapt behind it, and started pushing it towards the center of the room. A curious Max joined him in process.

"What are you doing?"

"Yo, help me with this. I need it over there."

"What the hell for?"

"Time's a factor, just shut up and help."

Max rolled her eyes, gripped the waist-high stand, and started dragging it towards the center. With a final tug and twist, it became a makeshift podium. Ross jumped on top, studied the view, then nodded with approval.

"Perfect. Now I need a chopstick."

"Huh?"

"A stick, a pencil, anything of the like."

Max glanced around the immediate area and spotted a small rod that had snapped off a sculpture. She plucked it from the floor debris and offered it to the feline.

"That'll work," Ross said and snatched it from Max.

"You're welcome."

"No time for decorum, got shit to do."

Max huffed. "You could have said *thanks* in the time it took you to explain why you didn't say *thanks*."

Ross sneered at his human companion, then focused on the quarrel upfront.

"So what's this all about, anyway?"

Ross reared back onto his hind legs and spread his arms like an orchestra conductor. "Max, my friend, I'm about to redefine the concept of thunder stealing."

Fio and Nifan continued to bicker with Jerry and Essien stoking the flames. Zoey and Perra traded bored glances as they suffered through an endless barrage of underhanded insults. Nifan queued up another jab, but the purple slivers of vessels exiting hyperspace caught her attention. The rest of the group followed her gaze as a large fleet of unknown origin blinked into orbit above the battered Terramesh. The dark blue ships resembled slivers of glacial ice, their smooth hulls reflecting the peripheral sunlight of Behemet.

"Who the hell are they?" Lord Essien said.

"Those are Byokane fighters," Nifan said with a puzzled tone. "What possible business do they have out here?"

Another fleet blinked out of hyperspace at the opposite side, filling the black with hundreds of battleships. Another fleet appeared, then another, and another, creating a giant amalgam of vessels surrounding the imploded mesh. Every race, creed, color, and grotesque mutation from around the galaxy, united as one for a mysterious calling.

Assault panels pinged to life as Boobybork and Durflock fleets exited hyperspace behind the ship. Migg's Ripper and Henry's fighter floated into view along the panoramic wall, each primed for battle. Flickers of charge snaked around the Suth'ra orbs above them.

Eyes widened and jaws slacked as a freakish swarm of ships filled the entire visual field, like heavy snow through a windshield. A palpable tension infected the bridge.

"What the hell is going on?" Fio said. "Why is everyone ignoring me?"

A clanking sound echoed around the chamber, hooking everyone's attention. They turned to find Ross banging the rod against the cube stand. Max stood nearby with hands in her pockets, looking like a bored teen at a family gathering. Ross resumed his readied position and cleared his throat.

"Welcome travelers," he said with a rumbling baritone. His voice penetrated the minds of every being in the system, current party included. "You have been summoned here as pawns and disciples, zealots and heretics, vassals of the one true god whose name is I. Behold! Gaze upon my visage and despair!"

Ross whipped the baton forward, prompting a blinding discharge from within the mesh. They recoiled and shielded their eyes as streaks of purple lightning danced around the assembled armada. The husk of the Terramesh glowed with an energy build that pulsed like a heartbeat. Fissures of light snaked across the surface like a cracking egg. The northern pole exploded with the force of a trillion nuclear warheads, hurling moon-sized chunks into the heavens. The resulting shockwave battered every ship in the system.

And then silence.

Every eye within a million miles locked onto the colossal chasm atop the Terramesh.

Ross grinned at Max while twirling the rod like a cocky drummer. "Here's something you don't see every day." He gripped the baton with both paws, dropped his fists to the stand, and started to lift.

Jaws fell and lungs emptied as a furry monolith sprouted from the chasm. The purple arm of a titanic monster spread its fingers and crashed into the rocky surface, hitting with the raw power of colliding planets. Another arm shot into the sky and smashed the opposite bank. Ebon claws the length of cities dug into the crust and lifted the creature from deep inside the fissure. The head of a giant purple ferret emerged from the void, housing jet black eyes the size of moons. The beast climbed out of the stony carapace and perched on top. Its massive tail swung through space and slapped the outer crust, flattening mountains and shaking the husk from pole to pole. The towering weasel emitted a deafening roar that made Godzilla's sound like a mouse sneeze. The titan reared onto its hind legs and loomed over the armada.

Back inside the bridge, a shared sense of shock and awe paralyzed the group. Nifan, Essien, Zoey, and Perra gawked at the giant ferret like frightened mannequins. Jerry leaned into the hologram feed and whispered to Fio.

"A giant *what?*" Fio said.

The feed abruptly ended.

Ross tossed the baton into the air, cracked his knuckles, then caught and held it like a guitar. Bands of light swirled around the ferret god to form a celestial banjo. The colossus gripped the neck and palmed the body, ready to drop some serious twang. Ross, the Fifth Force of Nature, resumed his address to the massive armada.

"Tremble before Tim the Destroyer of Worlds! I am the alpha and the omega, the giver and taker of life, the creator of all things, the almighty Banjo Ferret!" Ross raised a paw over his head and came down onto the rod with a rock star strum, as did the ferret god. The stellar banjo exploded into a flower of purple lightning and shattered every intercom in the system. A massive discharge enveloped the fleet, muting the glow of the nearby megastar.

When the light faded, the ferret was gone.

The Terramesh had returned to its imploded state.

The enormous armada floated in stunned silence.

Everyone turned to Ross, still perched upon the cube.

"Wait for it," he said with a playful uptick.

Lord Essien stuttered.

Nifan tried to form a coherent sentence.

"Wait for it."

Zoey traded glances between Ross and the mesh.

Perra tried to mime some understanding.

"Wait for it."

Off in the distance, a plasma streak ripped through the black. Another streak followed, then another, and another, zipping around the mesh like a meteor shower. A battleship exploded. Missiles screamed from launch tubes. Ion cannons flashed in response. Before long, the entire armada erupted into a heated battle.

"And *that* is how you start an intergalactic holy war." Ross stretched out the baton like a hot mic, then dropped it to the floor.

CHAPTER 16

The bridge of Nifan's stealth ship remained strangely quiet, despite the raging holy war in the background. A legion of warring vessels swarmed around the Terramesh husk, like bees around a massive hive. Random explosions bathed the interior with an orange sheen. The occasional strike on the exterior shield sent a wash of static around the ship.

But none of it mattered.

The wrath on Nifan's face filled the chamber with dread. Even Lord Essien gave her plenty of space to spontaneously combust, should it come to that. Clawed hands pulsed with pure venom. Heated breaths escaped a gaping mouth, like a panting gorilla. Cobalt eyes widened to a fury point that no one else in the room had ever witnessed. Her frenzied gaze tore into Ross, still sitting upon the cube.

The feline winked and smiled back.

"You underhanded son of a cock!" Nifan said. "That was *my* work! Mine and mine alone! How dare you steal it away like a common thief!"

Essien clutched her hand, but Nifan yanked it back. The shoulder of her dress slipped down her arm, but the hatred kept her from noticing. Strands of white hair unraveled and departed, giving her an

Einstein coiffure. Her crafted grace evaporated into a coked-out prom date as she rant-walked towards the feline.

Ross cocked an ear back.

"You just fucked with the wrong space bitch," she said in a grating voice. "I, Orantha Nifan, the goddamn Dossier, just annihilated 80 planets with a wave of my—"

"86," Ross said.

Nifan halted mid-step. "What?"

"86 planets. But hey, math is hard."

Nifan shrieked with rage and rushed at the feline.

Max leapt into action and tackled her from the side just before she reached Ross, sending them both crashing to the ground. Essien scurried over to help, but found herself in a Zoey head-lock. Max pinned Nifan to the floor, climbed on top, and started wailing on her face. Perra grabbed a table leg and hurried over to Zoey. Essien managed to flip Zoey off her back, only to receive a spinal smash from Perra. She fell to all fours, gasping and panting. Zoey scrambled to her feet and kicked Essien across the cheek, spurting blood and knocking her out cold. Max continued her windmill assault on Nifan's face. She reared back for another hit, but Perra nabbed her wrist.

"We still need her," Perra said.

Max nodded and climbed to her feet.

Nifan coughed and wheezed as blood poured from her nose and mouth. Her eye began to swell, darkening an ashy complexion. Red splatters stained her silky dress. She rolled off to the side and hacked bloody saliva onto the floor. Max loomed over Nifan with reddened fists, painting her with a sinister shadow.

"That was badass," Ross said as he trotted over.

Max studied her gory hands. "Thanks, I guess."

"You guess? What's wrong?"

"I dunno. Even under the circumstances, it feels wrong to hit a woman."

"But you *are* a woman."

Max glanced at her breasts, then grinned and squeezed them together. "Oh yeah. In that case, it felt fantastic."

Perra responded with a *don't want to know* head shake. She hooked Nifan by the armpits and pulled her to her feet. Nifan stumbled against a nearby wall and stamped it with red palm prints. She wiped her mouth on her forearm and glared back at Perra.

"You think you've won?"

"I think you got your ass kicked."

Nifan sneered in response, then spat a dollop of blood at her feet. "You forget your place, whore. You're on *my* ship with *my* rules. Tatia! Get—"

Zoey pinned Nifan against the wall and pressed a blade to her neck, one of the fruit carvers from the bar. "If the next words out of your filthy mouth aren't 'prep the freighter for departure,' then there won't be any more words."

Nifan scowled at the Mulgawat, then sighed.

The elevator ride down to the hangar reached a whole new level of awkwardness. Nifan stood front and center with wrists bound and hair unbound. She donned a mauled yet miffed expression. Zoey stood directly behind her, holding the blade at her throat. Perra stood to one side with Ross in her arms. The cat purred under a series of gentle strokes, as if nothing were amiss. Max stood on the other side. Her face carried a distressed expression and a few red splatters, like the lone survivor of a horror movie. Everyone, minus Ross, stared straight ahead while a pleasant melody played in the background. Ross stared intently at Nifan's face and batted at each drop of blood that fell from her nose.

"I'm going to murder you all," Nifan said.

The elevator dinged and the doors slid open, revealing the scuffed floor of the service bay tunnel. Zoey lowered the blade and nudged Nifan in the back. She floated into the corridor, doing her best to rekindle some swank beneath a battered exterior. Nifan led the group down a hallway and into the near-empty hangar. Tools and cargo boxes littered the floor, the remnants of a hasty departure. Plasma streaks and missiles zipped by the transparent barrier as Durflocks and Boobyborks battled over ferret allegiance. Nifan sighed and shook her head like a disappointed mother watching a sibling scuffle. Off to the far side, the tiny freighter rested in wait, detached from its shackles.

Out of nowhere, Migg and his Ripper tore through the barrier, filling the hangar with a fiery roar. The vessel swept around the room and clunked to the ground with a clumsy landing. Henry and his fighter followed suit, opting for a less than stellar entry. His triangular ship smacked the floor and skidded to a halt, spraying sparks and grinding metal. Both airlocks opened at the same time, revealing the tearful faces of rivals turned lovers. Henry and Migg ran to each other in the galactic equivalent of a soap opera reunion (sans slow motion). Migg's tiny legs blurred under his purple suit. Henry's beefy frame thumped the ground with each stride, his sunken eyes wet with heartache. They met in the empty space between ships. Henry dropped to his knees and Migg leapt into the embrace. They wept with joyful remorse.

"Aw," Perra said. "That's so sweet."

"Traitors!" Nifan said, sending a harsh echo around the chamber.

Henry and Migg flinched at the sudden shout, unaware of the company. Their sorrow morphed into disgust as they broke the embrace and stomped towards the group. Nifan hardened her stance as they closed in. Henry thundered to a stop and loomed over his master with a vicious gaze. Migg huffed and crossed his arms, his mustache wriggling with anger. Nifan stood tall, fighting to suppress a quivering lip. Henry heaved and panted like a rabid bull. He balled a fist, reared back, and hammered down with the full force of his mighty frame. Nifan recoiled from the hit, but found herself on the losing end of a giant middle finger.

"Fuuuuuuuuuuck you!" Henry said in his high-pitched squeaky voice.

Ross burst into laughter.

The rest snorted and snickered.

Henry waved his finger around the group, then turned away and tramped towards a small jump shuttle with Migg in tow. Hull thrusters ignited, lifting the ship onto pillars of blue flame. Henry glared through the viewport and flipped another finger before kicking the vessel through the barrier and disappearing into the black.

"Such an adorable couple," Perra said.

"Listen and listen well," Nifan said as she turned to face the group. Her brow tightened with rage. "The day may be yours, but a new war has begun. Your actions have opened wounds that cannot heal without a river of blood. Make no mistake, for each of you has signed a death warrant. I will not rest until I have looked each and every one of you in the eye and thrust my blade into—"

Zoey nailed her chin with a savage uppercut. The strike took Nifan off her feet and sprayed a mist of blood. She flew through the air like a ragdoll and smacked the hangar floor. Her brain tapped out before flesh hit metal, leaving her body in a twisted pile.

"Oh, she's definitely killing you last," Ross said.

"I imagine so," Zoey said as she shook the sting from her knuckles.

"Why not just cap them both right now?"

"Can't," Perra said. "If we're going to survive this, we need the full support of Loken and the PCDS."

"Exactly," Zoey said. "Killing a nut job like Halim is one thing, but capping a kingpin is grounds for banishment. Like Nifan said, the PCDS has no jurisdiction. Our rep is the only thing that keeps us breathing."

A missile slammed into the shield, jostling the ship. Max yelped as she stumbled to the floor and smacked her bum. Ross flared his stance like a nervy skydiver. Zoey fought for balance, then turned to Perra.

"Spin up for departure, jump drive and all."

Perra nodded and jogged towards the freighter.

Max and Ross followed.

Zoey took one final look around the hangar and brought up the rear.

A no-look wall slap closed the airlock as Zoey bounded into the ship. She snatched a pair of plasma pistols from a wall locker and hurried into the cockpit, tossing a skeptical gaze at Max and Ross along the way.

"Shit, that's right," Max said.

"Mhmm," Ross said. "You still need to reset this whole charade."

Max glanced around the cargo bay. "I guess I could just run into a wall or something."

"Not now, dumbass. You're still on Nifan's cruiser. You could wake up as a dock worker."

"Or a sex slave."

"Yeah, to Henry."

Max grimaced and shivered.

"First things first, let the orange spark plugs get us the hell out of here. Once we are free and clear, we can worry about your next log jammer."

"You mean log sawer."

"No, I do not."

Ross trotted up the corridor and into the cockpit where Zoey and Perra speed-prepped for launch. Max adjusted her wayward thong in a very unsexy way and followed Ross into the cabin. She dropped into the passenger seat behind Perra and strapped in for the ride.

"Don't get too comfy, Maxine," Zoey said while flicking some overhead switches. "Once we're out of this mess, we're dumping you at the nearest port."

"But we saved your lives," Max said.

"No, the fuzzball saved us. You're just the filthy Veiled Trader who wailed on a bitch who deserved it." She paused to lock eyes with Max. "We're letting you live as a kindness, so best take it as such and shut your trap."

Max turned to Ross. "No respect, dude."

Ross huffed. "Does *shut your trap* mean *talk to the cat* in your brain? I swear, it's like you're genetically programmed to undermine your own self-interests."

Perra chuckled and grinned at Zoey. "I like the cat. Can we keep 'em?"

Zoey shrugged and slapped the thrusters icon. "As long as he doesn't turn into a giant purple ferret."

The tiny freighter rumbled to life and hovered on pillars of blue flame. The landing gear retracted as the ship angled towards the entry barrier. Random debris bounced around the hangar. The silky fabric of Nifan's soiled dress fluttered in the exhaust. She began to stir on the ground as Zoey ignited the main engines and kicked the vessel forward. It sliced through the barrier and into the chaotic battle already in progress.

Durflock and Boobybork ships swarmed the area, firing upon each other with a cold ferocity. Suth'ra orbs peppered the battle, zotting every unfortunate vessel that got in their way. A torrent of missiles screamed by and slammed into a cruiser, forcing Zoey to barrel roll away and push towards the Terramesh. Gasps filled the cabin as the full scene came into view. The incursion carried a weight of anarchy, a dog-eat-dog slaughter where any kill was a good kill. After all, the omnipotent Banjo Ferret had appeared to the proletariat, injecting the Ferretian ships with a reckless ferocity.

"Holy mother of Tim," Perra said.

"I don't have a mother," Ross said.

"What the hell are you?" Zoey said, her curiosity briefly skirting the desire to live. An ion blast clipped the freighter, causing her to adjust course and dive beneath a warship.

"It's a long story."

"Are you a god?" Perra said.

"Do you really want to have this chat right now?"

"Ross!" Max said with a hint of bother. "When someone asks you if you're a god, you say *yes!*"

Ross turned to Max, then howled with laughter.

Max followed suit, shedding tears and slapping knees.

Zoey tossed Perra a puzzled glance before whipping the ship around a squadron.

Perra leaned forward and scanned the chaos. "Can we not jump to a peripheral or something?"

"No," Zoey said as she darted through a dogfight. "Too many

ships, can't risk a collision. We need to reach the edge first, then we can—"

A giant explosion rocked the ship from behind, jostling the frame and shaking everyone inside. Alerts sounded and sirens blared, filling the cockpit with blinking red lights. A debris field zipped by the viewport. Perra tapped across the console to assess the damage.

"Not our hit," Zoey said, pointing to a chunk of severed wing. "Secondary impact."

"That explains the lack of target lock," Perra said.

Zoey silenced the shrieking alarms while Perra scanned the console output.

"Critical systems okay. Guidance shook, but functional. Shit! Jump drive offline."

"Screw the rest, we need the jump."

"On it." Perra unbuckled her harness, leapt to her feet, and shot down the corridor.

Max also sprang into action. She unbuckled her harness, hooking Zoey's attention.

"Where the hell do you think you're going?"

"To help Perra. I'm her intern, remember?"

"And why would she remember that?" Ross said.

Max sighed. "You know, this whole thing is a perplexing pain in the crack. I'm going to be so happy when I pass out and they're my friends again."

Zoey replied with a narrowed gaze.

"Just ignore her," Ross said, adding an eye roll. "But on the other hand, Max does have machining experience with M-class freighters. She can actually help."

Zoey fought through her hesitation, then nodded.

Max grinned and hurried down the tunnel.

Ross leapt into the co-pilot chair and spun around a few times before taking a seat. He dug his claws into the leather and started grooming his chest.

Zoey grumbled. "I just had those reupholstered."

"So bill me."

"And where should I send the invoice? 42 Ferret Lane in the Imagod System?"

"Shut up, Ray."

"Ray?"

"It's a *Ghostbusters* reference."

"What's Ghost—"

"Stop yapping and mind the road. It was funny the first time."

Back in the engine room, Perra snapped a tool belt to her waist and rushed around a tangled mess of components. The cramped quarters housed sophisticated machinery inside a military-grade frame, not the easiest to service. Perra poked and prodded the jump drive, a complex retrofit that utilized the tiny freighter shell. She had built it herself, but even she struggled to make sense of the structure.

Max sprinted through the cargo bay and swung around the machine room doorframe. "Yo!"

Perra yelped and dropped the wrench in her hand. She palmed her chest and gasped for breath as the tool clanked to a rest upon the grimy floor. "Jeez, give me a heart attack why don't you."

"Sorry, just here to help."

"Help?" Perra reached down and snatched the wrench from the floor. "What makes you think you can help?"

"Because we—" Max huffed. "I worked with a friend in an M-class freighter."

Zoey banked hard, tossing Max and Perra into the wall. They grimaced and stumbled to regain balance. Perra gave Max a leery look, then sighed.

"Fine," she said. "Grab a flashlight from the—"

Max plucked a flashlight from a nearby cubby before she could finish the sentence.

Perra raised an eyebrow, then got back to work.

They tackled the problem head-on with Perra checking the housing while Max studied the feeds. Panels and parts rained to the floor as they dove deeper and deeper into the system. Random banks and turns bruised elbows and cued choice curses. Perra unlatched a wiring panel and groaned after checking all the connections. Max's legs swung from a narrow cubby like a botched prison escape. Perra wiped her greasy brow and sighed.

"Got it!" Max said, her voice muffled from inside.

Perra perked and rushed over. "What did you find?"

"Looks like the primary routing circuit got cooked, likely a blast surge."

"Shit. We don't have a replacement for that line."

Max's legs slacked.

Perra barked with frustration and kicked the wall.

Inside the compartment, Max glanced around a mess of wires and feeds. She recalled the time in the Ripper when she and Ross restored the life support system. Max chewed on her cheek while studying a complex array of connectors. Moments later, a sudden realization widened her eyes. "Yo! Can Zoey pilot with one engine?"

Perra tilted her head. "I'm listening."

"The drives use different feeds and voltage, but rely on the same connections. The build won't be as strong, but at least you can power it up. This assumes, of course, that Zoey can keep us alive with one can."

Perra nodded while running a mental calculation, then grunted and clapped with approval. "Make it happen. I'll let Zoey know."

Max grinned and began rewiring the components. Perra relayed the plan, caught some flack, pushed back with the threat of a sex embargo, and won over Zoey. Max completed the task and shimmied out from the cubby. The drive meters pinged with power and the jump core started to replenish its energy. The gauges climbed slower than usual, but did so at a steady pace. Max pumped her fists and met eyes with an impressed Perra.

"Nicely done, Earthling."

"Thanks. I trained under the best."

They indulged in a crisp high five before getting tossed into the wall again.

"On that note," Perra said, "let's get the hell out of here."

Perra rushed out of the engine room and up towards the cockpit with Max in tow. They staggered through the cargo bay as if drunk on a sailboat. After a few slips and bumps, they arrived at the cockpit corridor.

Perra gripped the wall and turned to Max. "Follow me," she said and ducked inside the guest cabin.

Max nodded, then hooked the frame and swung inside. A smile lifted her cheeks as she glanced around the familiar quarters, but the grin inverted when Perra buried a fist into her stomach. Max dropped to the cold metal floor like a sack of rocks. As she gasped for breath, Perra retrieved a pair of handcuffs and latched one end to Max's wrist. She yanked her over to the bed and latched the other end to the sturdy frame. Max coughed and wheezed before locking eyes with a resolute Perra.

"What the hell?"

"Thanks for the patch, but I still don't trust you." Perra stood to leave.

"Wait! Wait!" Max said, still trying to catch her breath. "Just do me one favor."

Perra crossed her arms.

"Could you, um ... punch me in the face as hard as you can?"

Perra snort-chuckled. "With pleasure." She reared back and clocked Max across the cheek, knocking her out cold.

Max hung from the frame like a hazing gone wrong.

Perra returned to the cockpit and plucked Ross from the co-pilot seat. Under a hail of hisses and scratches, she tossed him into the guest cabin with Max and locked the door. The jump drive pinged with full charge as she plopped back into her rightful seat. After a hasty re-buckle, she concluded with a heavy sigh.

"Strong work," Zoey said.

"Thanks," Perra said with a wearied tone that screamed *so done with this adventure.*

A final dip and dive opened a clean patch of black.

"About damn time," Zoey said.

She slapped the jump icon and the freighter disappeared into a sliver of purple light.

CHAPTER 17

Max awoke after a long and needed sleep. The soft sheets of his familiar guest cabin bed drew a wide smile on his face. Lazy blinks and lip-smacks greeted the new day. A curious smell wrinkled his nose, likely his own funk. Whatever the new world, he didn't care in the slightest. He had made it home, and that was more than enough after a nutty jaunt from Yankar.

A shifting leg nudged a mass at the end of the bed. Max tucked his chin and glanced down to find a snoring pile of orange fur. He smiled and started to rise for a morning pet, but a mystery force halted his ascent. A quick assessment uncovered a pair of fluffy pink handcuffs binding his wrist to the bed frame. He studied the device, gave it a few yanks, and came to the annoying conclusion that he needed some help (and perhaps an explanation).

"Guanchia," he said, prompting the cabin door to slide open. "A little help, please?"

"Just a tick," Perra said from afar. She moseyed inside a short time later with a pink key in hand and a sly grin on her face. A thin set of jammies clung to her body, leaving little to the imagination.

"Um," Max said, surprised by the visual.

"I figured you might need this." Perra took a seat on the bed and unlocked the cuffs. "I would have taken care of this sooner, but I didn't want to wake you. After the day we had, you earned some undisturbed rest."

Max locked eyes with Perra as his teenage brain fought to keep his gaze above her chest. The temptation proved too great, so he turned away and stared at the foot of the bed. Ross had stood upright with a Cheshire grin, evoking some mild concern.

"Uh ... g'morning?" Max said.

"Depends on where this goes."

Max sighed and grimaced, which shifted his attention to a sore cheek. He massaged his jaw and turned back to Perra. "Man, you really clocked me hard."

"What do you mean?"

"My jaw, it's still sore."

Perra smirked. "Well, yeah, you worked it pretty hard last night."

"I worked it ... what?"

"You went the full distance, Earthman. I'm actually quite impressed. Hell, Zoey is still walking with a limp."

The realization hit Max like a glittery freight train. "You mean to tell me that we ..."

"Don't get me wrong, it was weird at first. But once we hit our stride, it was oddly satisfying. However, it needs to remain a one-time thing. We are family and that comes first. I think we just needed the stress relief."

Max glanced over to Ross, who could barely contain his snickering.

"But anyway, I'm glad you're feeling well. There's some hot breakfast waiting when you're ready." Perra kissed his cheek and smiled before rising from the bed. She sauntered out of the cabin while twirling the frizzy pink cuffs around her finger. The door closed behind her.

Max facepalmed himself and collapsed into the bed.

Ross chuckled for a bit and ended with a sigh. "So yeah, about last night. You and the ladies got—"

"No, stop. I don't want to hear it. This is weird enough without one of your snarky recaps."

"Weird? In what way?"

"Dude, how would you feel if you banged your sister?"

"But they're not your sisters."

"They *are* my sisters. I just ... nevermind, I don't want to talk about it."

Ross shrugged. "Suit yourself."

Max writhed and groaned as a wave of raunchy images flooded his mind, as if forced to rehash a taboo sex dream. He shivered away the visuals, wiped his forehead, and took a measured breath. Despite the upsetting situation, a happy reality dawned upon him. Max lifted the sheets and greeted the return of his precious dangle. "Good to have you back, buddy."

"I didn't go anywhere," Ross said.

"I was talking to my penis," Max said, then immediately regretted the statement.

"Too easy," Ross said, then dove into a morning groom.

Max tossed the sheets aside and hoisted his aching body to a seated position. He stared at his slumped reflection in the opposite wall. Another groan escaped his chest, forcing him to look away and hunt for a distraction.

"Fikarek," he said, rendering the back wall transparent. An ocean of stars filled the plane, along with a handful of distant galaxies. The vessel was deep in the black, far away from anything of consequence. He grinned and left the wall as is, savoring some much-needed peace.

Lifting to his feet, Max strolled over to the hygiene panel and started to address an array of lingering smells. He took his merry time getting ready in order to appreciate the very nature of getting ready. Simple tasks gained new meaning after experiencing life as a grubby caveman. A spritz on the pits created the same pleasure as a whiff of coffee. Slipping into a clean set of garments raised goosebumps on his skin. Teasing hair into a deliberate style prompted the same care and attention as a master chef concocting a royal feast. With order restored and brain rebooted, he tapped the wall panel and reset the room to its pre-coitus configuration.

Max departed the cabin with Ross in tow and paused to glance around a near-empty cargo bay. Perra sat at a small table in the rear, sipping on a mug of coffee while reading the output of her comdev. She had changed into her usual punky attire, a buckled and leather ensemble stripped from the pages of Rebel Weekly.

"G'morning, jackhammer," Zoey said from behind. She ruffled his hair as she passed (and yes, walked with a slight limp). The upper half of her pilot suit swung from her waist, revealing a jet black tank top that matched her choppy hair. She snatched a pastry from the breakfast table and plopped into the chair across from Perra.

Perra eyed Max and waved him over. "C'mon, you've got to be starving."

Max wandered over to the table and took a seat. They all exchanged timid glances as he grabbed a plate and filled it with a variety of morsels. A rare moment of shyness floated around the group, like a family dinner after an unexpected reveal. As Max lifted his first bite, Ross leapt into the last of four chairs and cleared his throat.

"Time to address the elephant in the room," Ross said.

"What's an elephant?" Zoey said through a mouthful of noms.

"Doesn't matter. The point is, you three kept me up with all the moaning and the pounding and the hollering."

"Max and I already talked about it," Perra said. "We're cool, so no need to worry. Won't happen again."

"Thank you," Ross said. "I just want to make sure that I will not have to endure your passionate shouts and vulgar expletives again. A kitty has to sleep."

Perra shied away and took another bite.

Ross turned to Zoey. "And as for you, Miss Hit-It-Like-You-Mean-It, I never want to hear your growling demands, ceaseless wall thumps, or the wet slaps of flesh on flesh ever again."

"Noted," Zoey said with a hint of *wrap it up, fuzzball*.

"Thank you for your candor," Ross said. "Regardless, I am happy that you three were able to resolve the obvious tension and get it out of your systems."

"Me too," Perra said.

"Ditto," Zoey said.

They all turned to Max, who had buried his face in his hands.

"What's wrong?" Perra said.

Max slid his palms down his face and plunked them on the table. He shook his head at nothing in particular before glaring at Ross. "Thanks for that. I could have done without the erotic review, you furry little prick."

Zoey and Perra glanced at each other.

"Erotic ... huh?" Zoey said.

"So we shared a moment of raw passion. It's not like we did anything wrong. Ross can poke all the fun as he wants, but I'm glad we alleviated some sexual tension."

All eyes widened.

Zoey covered her mouth.

Perra cringed and dropped her jaw. "Are you saying that you, um, *climaxed* during the fight?"

Max stammered and shifted his gaze. "Um ..."

"Dude, we beat the stuffing out of each other. Things got heated over the escape, we exchanged some choice words, and things escalated. How exactly is that sexual?"

"But, you said that I worked my jaw last night."

"Yeah, you barked insults the entire time."

"But, Zoey is limping."

"Yeah, you tackled her over a crate."

"But, the pink handcuffs."

"We had to restrain you with *something*. And now you know a little about our private time."

"But, you said it needs to stay a one-time thing."

"Duh. That's not something we want to do again."

A dreadful silence infected the room as Zoey and Perra leered at Max like an outed pervert. A palpable shame hung between them for what seemed like an eternity. Max, having no clue how to rectify the situation, opted to stutter-panic while shaking like a nude Sherpa. With pressure mounting, Ross decided to intervene with a sudden burst of laughter.

"Gotcha!" he said, instantly diffusing the tension.

Perra groaned and thumped the table.

Zoey shook her head at the feline. "So not funny."

"It's a little funny," Ross said.

Max chuckled through sheer relief, then eyed Ross with a subtle gaze that read *you son of a whore!*

Ross replied with a head tilt that conveyed *you brought it on yourself, jackass. You're welcome, by the way.*

Perra snickered her way to a heavy sigh.

Zoey smirked and plucked another pastry.

Max mumbled some curses to the ceiling.

"So what's the plan?" Perra said.

"Well, the Council of Loken isn't going to do much until Nifan mounts an attack. We can inform them, but they can't protect us."

"Should we inform the PCDS? The org is unbound and we're their top couriers. We represent a certain investment value. They could offer some regional support."

Zoey thought for a moment, then sighed. "No, too risky. We compete indirectly with the Veiled Traders. All it takes is one corrupt client. Jai learned that the hard way."

"We can't go home, either. They'd anticipate it."

"We need a place to lay low until Nifan makes a move."

"What about Gamon?"

Zoey shook her head. "Durangoni is way too busy. Even if we did everything right, a curious snoop could botch the entire thing. Distance is also a factor. Too many jumps, too many sniffers."

"Who do we know in the quadrant?"

"Hmm ... I think Nimmith still works the Milky Way."

"He's dead."

"Really? How?"

"I'll give you three guesses, but you'll only need one."

Zoey grunted. "He did love those chainsaws."

Max perked up. "Wait, we're still in the Milky Way?"

"Yeah. Why?"

Max spread his arms and grinned.

Perra perked up and turned to Zoey.

Zoey scoffed and rolled her eyes. "Are you kidding me? What are we going to do, hide in his mom's basement?"

"I have my own place, thank you very much."

"A door to the basement doesn't count."

"No, it's not a ... doesn't matter. Listen, they're looking for The Omen, right? Not The Omen's sad little Earthling friend. I'm invisible."

"Not unless they raid the Suth'ra."

"If they raid the nerd brigade," Ross said, "then you're all fucked."

"You mean *we're* all fucked."

"No, I do not."

Zoey glared at the feline. "What the hell are you?"

Perra whipped a wide-eyed gaze to her lover, shouting *don't anger the fur god!*

Ross glanced at his chest, then back to Zoey. "A cyborg cat, last time I checked."

"You know what I mean. Do you have any skin in this game or will you just conjure a giant marmot the next time things get weird?"

"Weasel."

"What?"

"Ferrets are weasels, not marmots."

Zoey leaned forward and crossed her arms on the table. "Thank you for the biology lesson, Professor Prick. But you still haven't answered the question."

"Just saying, if I wanted the universe to worship a giant groundhog, I would have appeared to that drunken bastard as a giant groundhog."

Zoey thumped her forehead on the table.

Max sighed. "Dude, just tell them."

Ross lowered his gaze. His jowls shifted back and forth as he pondered an answer. "Let's just say that I'm helping *you* by helping *him*. I can wield a cosmic influence, but not directly. As long as Max is safe, then you are safe."

"And what makes the Earthling so special?" Perra said, then turned to Max. "No offense."

"He's not," Ross said. "Not in the slightest. I mean, the guy is potently un-special. There are pieces of metal in this very room worth more than him."

Max rolled his eyes.

"However," Ross said, adding a weighted pause. "He's my best friend."

The declaration caught Max off-guard. His jaw slacked a bit as he met eyes with his longtime companion.

"So ask yourself," Ross said. "How far would you go to protect your best friend?"

A heavy silence fell upon the room. Zoey smiled at Perra as her eyes began to tear. She lowered her gaze to the table and thought for a moment. After careful consideration, she glanced around the group and offered a slight nod.

"Earth it is."

* * *

Battle debris floated around the Terramesh like a cloud of suspended snow. Large chunks of mangled hulls bumped through an ocean of shrapnel. The cold vacuum of space had snuffed out the remaining flickers, leaving a lifeless farrago of war waste. Clumps of rubbish began to coalesce under the combined gravity of the imploded worlds, flattening into an enormous ring of trash.

Nifan's stealth ship floated on the outskirts as the sole survivor. Or rather, the last vessel not to explode or bugger off. Hunks of debris wandered into the external shield and vaporized on impact, like flies on a bug zapper. The cruiser interior mirrored the exterior with shattered sculptures and broken glasses littering the floor. A tattered couch faced the transparent wall with missing cushions and abundant claw marks. Nifan and Lord Essien filled the remaining pillows, their faces battered and clothes bloodied. They gazed upon the devastation with lips clenched and arms crossed. Essien sighed and turned to

Nifan.

"It really was a thoughtful gift."

"Don't patronize me."

* * *

Perra tapped a sequence of commands into her comdev, then dropped it face-up on the breakfast table. A hologram rendition of the MW-9225 solar system pieced together and floated above the surface. A yellow dwarf star anchored the center with eight planets orbiting around it, four rocky and four gaseous. Panels of atmo data scrolled beside the feed. Zoey and Perra studied the traffic protocols as Max glanced around the familiar image with a goofy smile. Ross watched the orbital animation with his flattened head hovering just below the table ledge. He batted at Neptune every time it swung around.

"We can get there in a couple of jumps," Perra said. "But, remember that this is a controlled system. We have to taxi in from the perimeter, which extends our approach by a poch, maybe more. That's a lot of scan time to get noticed."

Zoey tapped on Earth, which blinked and zoomed into gridded detail. The planet rotated on a tilted axis, outlining oceans and continents. Vessel icons swarmed around ports as freighters queued for direct entry. "This is all Federation, which means we can use a supplier code to jump straight to the pole." She pointed to a trader zone over Greenland. "See there? That entire area is a jump harbor."

"That should work."

"Think you can get an entry code?"

"I don't see why not."

"Gravy, let's get to it then." Zoey nabbed another pastry and strolled towards the cockpit. "I'm going to plot our first jump. Let me know when you have that code."

"Will do." Perra swiped her comdev from the breakfast table, killing the feed. "Get your fill while you can," she said to Max. "We're cloaking the beacon and won't stop again until we touch down at your place."

"Um, okay," Max said, somewhat confused.

Ross rolled his eyes. "She means *eat the rest of this shit and clean off the table.*"

Perra click-pointed at Ross and sauntered away.

"Then why not just say that?"

"Because she's polite and you're dense."

Max frowned at the feline, then plucked a nibble from a random plate and tossed it down his gullet. Perra ducked into the main cabin and closed the door behind her, leaving them to the dull hum of the main engines. Max continued to snack on the mystery morsels while Ross glanced around the cargo bay.

"You know what this means, right?" Ross said.

Max chewed through another piece while staring at the table surface. "It means I might never come back. It means that, um ... that all of this will go away."

"Like on Yankar. Do you remember what I said? Never shift in a world you don't want to—"

"To live on for the rest of my life. I know."

"Then why did you suggest Earth?"

Max sighed and locked eyes with Ross. "Because they're my family. I love them both and want them to be safe."

"But you wouldn't be around to assure it."

"This version of me would. We had the same encounter at the Terramesh, so he should know what's up. He won't remember the trip to Earth, but so what? Zoey will explain it to him after a few calming slaps."

"She is tender like that."

"They'll be fine. And even if I wake up in an old world with old problems, at least I did right by them in this one. That's enough of a reason. It's enough for me." Max sighed and plucked another morsel. "Who knows, maybe I'll get lucky and shift back."

"But the odds of that are—"

"Never tell me the odds."

They shared a muted chuckle as a somber haze infected the

room. Max finished off the remaining noms and cleared the table. Ross caught up on some grooming, but paused at random intervals to reflect on the mood. Max scanned the cargo bay and smiled at all the dents and scratches he could link with fond memories. His chest raised and lowered with a heavy sigh before turning back to Ross.

"By the way, what's the current shift? I haven't noticed anything weird."

"Oh, um ... platypuses don't exist."

"Huh, interesting. Wonder why."

"Are you kidding? As if they made sense to begin with. They're the evolutionary equivalent of a cough-sneeze."

The main cabin door slid open, hooking their attention. Perra emerged with a big smile and a slip of paper in hand. "Gamon for the win," she said, adding lewd gesture before disappeared into the cockpit corridor.

Max secured the table and chairs, then followed her with Ross prancing behind.

Perra entered the cockpit, kissed the top of Zoey's head, and slapped the paper onto the console. "One of Gamon's cohorts has a convoy in route, three separate codes. He was able to merge down and reclassified the third as an M-class freighter."

Zoey grinned. "Strong work, my love."

Perra plopped into the co-pilot seat and buckled in.

Max strapped in behind her with Ross assuming the lap nap position.

Zoey entered the code, which pinged with confirmation and cued a hologram panel of jump protocols. She validated the trader zone coordinates, powered the drive, and turned to the Earthling. "You ready to go home?"

Max mustered a half-grin and nodded. "I guess so."

Ross began to snore as Zoey thumped the jump icon.

The drive swelled with an energy build and peaked with a flash of purple light.

CHAPTER 18

The tiny freighter blinked out of hyperspace just outside of Neptune's orbit. The blue planet hung inside the viewport like a rearview ornament. Triton floated in from the side, its pastel sheen serving as a stark contrast. Even with billions of miles between him and home, Max stared at the image with an odd mixture of assurance and reluctance.

"First jump complete," Zoey said as she started prep on the supplier jump.

Perra turned to Max. "This will take a little while if you want to stretch your legs."

Max glanced down at the snoring kitty in his lap, then smiled at Perra. "I'm good, thanks."

She returned the smile and refocused on helping Zoey.

Max glanced around the cockpit, taking mental notes of every switch and panel. He watched Zoey and Perra relay instruction back and forth like skilled dancers. Their voices trailed away, trapped inside a hazy echo, retreating further and further until the image crumbled. Max took a long and steady breath, then wiped his welling eyes on a sleeve.

"Coms up, beacon masked, let's get this party started." Zoey flicked an overhead switch and hailed the local port authority. "M-class freighter 687-B3 to transit."

"Go ahead, M-class," a static voice said.

"Requesting merchant clearance to jump site E2. Access code 922479."

"Stand by."

Perra crossed her fingers as they awaited a reply.

"Access granted. Jump when ready to subsite 14."

"Thank you, transit."

Zoey and Perra smirked and bumped fists.

"Seriously," Perra said. "How many times has Gamon saved our asses?"

"I lost count a long time ago," Zoey said while tapping coordinates into the console.

"When this is over, we should plan an extended stay at Durangoni and bring him a proper gift."

"Agreed."

An onset of sniffles hooked their attention. They turned to Max, who was on the verge of an ugly cry. A snot bubble expanded and contracted, accenting his puffy eyes and red cheeks. He frowned like a clown-for-hire with a backlog of bad life decisions.

"I feel ya, Earthman," Zoey said. "If we had to return to Mulgawat, I'd be a sniveling wreck too." She turned back to the console and thumped the jump icon, prompting a sliver of purple light to engulf the ship.

* * *

Nifan and Lord Essien wheezed and cackled over their seventh martinis. Essien stared at the ceiling while stretched across the tattered couch. Nifan stood at the bar, wobbling a bit as she topped off a beverage. The laughter subsided with a pair of heavy sighs.

"I had totally forgotten about that jackhole," Essien said.

"Those chins, man. They stuck out for days," Nifan said as she stumbled back to the couch. She swish-plopped into the cushions, spilling a bit of her drink.

Lord Essien lifted her legs and draped them over Nifan's lap. "I kinda feel bad about Jai."

Nifan grunted. "What for? I never understood what you saw in that green, greeny green, meathead man thing."

"I treated him like shit."

"Since when do you care about the peons?"

"I don't. But he was like, super-duper loyal, which is so hard to find in a minion these days. Who knows, maybe he survived."

Nifan raked a tipsy gaze over the Terramesh ruination, then fluttered her lips. "Doubtful."

"Am I pretty?"

Nifan puckered her face and turned to Essien. "Sweetie, you're the prettiest—" She dry heaved, then patted a belch from her chest. "Sorry ... you're the prettiest pretty lady I have ever seen, ever."

Essien grinned, then scrunched her brow. "The room is starting to spin."

"Then spin with it, lover." Nifan swirled a spill from her glass. "We ain't got nowhere to be but here."

"I'm just, um, I'm just gonna close my eyes for a bit. I'm not sleeping, promise."

"Do what you need to."

"Ugh, that just makes it worse."

Nifan groaned like a chore-laden teen and dropped her head on the rear cushion. "Fucking ferret."

* * *

Jai Ferenhal sat upon a small boulder inside a dank cave while overlooking a pitiful campfire, again. The mound of dried algae he burned required constant attention. With no sticks to account for, he poked at it with the toe of his dirty boot. Every jostle belched a cloud of tiny embers. A column of white smoke climbed to the ceiling and slithered along the ridges, like an inverted haunted house.

A muted rumble filled the cavern, prompting a sigh and grimace.

Jai glanced over to a massive heap of dried algae, enough to feed the fire for an entire fortnight. Soon after, a rolling mound of flesh skidded to a halt and puked another batch onto the pile.

"Is this enough, friend?!" Phil said.

Jai eyed the flesh pile, then the algae pile, then the flesh pile, then closed his eyes for a moment to mourn the loss of peace. "No. Still need more."

"Okie dokie artichokie!" Phil sprouted a tendril, saluted Jai, then raced out of the cavern.

* * *

With a final flash of light, the familiar blue-green dome of Earth filled the viewport. Despite the circumstance, Max grinned as he walked his gaze through the icy mountains of Greenland and down to the lush forests of North America. An endless bank of clouds swirled atop the deep blue seas. The vision captured his mind, as if plucked from the pages of an astronomy textbook.

"So this is home," Perra said.

"Yup," Max said. "That's my rock."

"Did you miss it?"

Max thought for a moment. "In some ways."

"I know what you mean," Zoey said with a slight nod. "Mulgawat isn't my favorite place in the 'verse, but there are some creature comforts I miss."

"Like a good grompum stew," Perra said.

"With a side of toasted miriash," Zoey said.

The ladies groaned at the delicious memory.

Max sighed to himself.

Numerous supply ships queued up over the Greenland port entrance, awaiting their turns to descend through the atmosphere. Zoey joined the line. A small station managed the merchant traffic, like a tollbooth jockey floating in orbit. Before long, the ship overlooked the Earthly landscape with nobody to block the view. A sizzle of static filled the cabin, followed by a sharp ping and a robotic voice.

"M-class freighter 687-B3 cleared for entry."

"Copy," Zoey said, then powered the main engines.

The ship glided through the upper atmosphere, leaving a trail of flame in its wake. The cockpit bumped and rattled as orange streaks flooded the viewport. The rumbling ceased soon after, leaving them to the snowy peaks of Greenland. Patches of actual green appeared as they neared the coast, giving way to a boundless plane of blue. Merchant vessels gathered around the large southern port, used mostly as a routing station. A distinct lack of shiny hulls gave the area a transient presence, like the shipping docks of old.

"What's the city again?" Perra said.

"Albuquerque," Max said.

"Going to have to spell that for me."

Max grinned. "Haven't had to do that for a while. A, l, b, u, q—"

"There it is, got it." Perra studied a regional data panel. "Hmm, looks like the closest supplier port is in Denver. We can park there and take the maglev rail south. Straight shot, 20 minutes."

"What's a minute?" Zoey said.

"Like, 50 ticks. Half a boink, basically."

Zoey huffed. "Earthlings and their imperial nonsense." She turned to Max with a mocking stare. "You can join the rest of the universe anytime you want."

"Two minutes is a *boink*?" Max said.

"Yeah, why?"

"Nothing, just oddly relevant."

Perra entered their final destination as Zoey confirmed the relay with the Greenland port. They sailed past the com towers and over the ocean, retaining a comfortable cruising altitude all the way to Denver. Cities and ports littered the surface as they pushed into the mainland. Toronto stuck out as a bustling metropolis with floating parks and gleaming skyscrapers, drawing *oohs* and *ahhs* from the Mulgawats. Ross continued to snore in Max's lap.

Perra located a long-term storage facility that accepted non-Federation funds. Knowing the dangers of their career choice, Zoey and Perra planned ahead and distributed their wealth around the cosmos. They deposited income inside a variety of institutions, everything from the PCDS Galactic Credit Union to the hollow floor panel of a cash-only moon rental. Non-Federation banks offered the one-two punch of support and secrecy. Criminal factions adored them, but all it took was a nasty local conflict to wipe out every cent. The Terramesh implosion snuffed out hundreds of these banks, generating a tidal wave of instability.

Zoey cruised over the Denver outskirts and descended on a grungy warehouse facility that resembled an RV park. A scruffy chap named Rufus guided them into the bowels of the main hangar, which offered 24-hour security at a higher premium. They paid, tipped well, and started locking down the ship. Perra secured the engine room as Zoey cleared the cabins. She emerged with a duffle bag of personal items and dropped it at the base of a wall locker.

"Double and triple check your gear," Zoey said to Max. "Don't leave anything behind that can trace you home."

Max lifted a half-full backpack. "Not much to trace."

"The ship will disinfect itself, so don't worry about any biomarkers."

"Bio what?"

"Stains," Ross said. "You are a teenage boy after all."

"I'm a young adult, thank you."

"Oh, does that mean fewer stains?"

Max opened his mouth to reply, but huffed and walked towards the airlock.

Perra emerged from the engine room with a small bag of tools and gadgets. She added them to the duffle bag as Zoey retrieved the plasma pistols from the wall locker and slipped them into a specialized pouch. Perra grabbed the duffle and swung it over her neck, adjusting for comfort. Zoey placed the pouch into her sling pack along with a few more items. After a final sweep, the group gathered around the airlock.

"There's a maglev station on the next block," Perra said. "Easy walk."

Zoey turned to Max. "Anything we should know?"

"About what?"

"About Earth, nimrod. This is your home. Any cultural or social issues we should know about?"

"Oh, right. Um ... last time I checked, everybody hated everybody."

"Standard tribal crap," Ross said. "Just sneer at anyone who doesn't look like you and you'll fit right in."

"Baseline bigotry, got it."

The group exited the freighter one by one, dropping to a grimy concrete floor. Floodlights overhead filled the hangar with an ominous glow, like a gangster bar on an epic scale. With the vessel locked up and powered down, Perra closed the airlock door and disabled the access panel. She gave the boxy craft a loving pat.

"Be good, baby. We'll be back for you later."

The jaunt back to Albuquerque was largely uneventful, aside from a social incident involving a blue-haired scientist and his yellow-shirted grandson. Max was caught staring, which provoked the scientist to mercilessly berate him. The grandson moaned with anxiety as the scientist belched an array of expletives. After all was said and done, Max tried to explain why it was one of the greatest moments of his life. Zoey and Perra refused to accept such a stupid premise and the discussion stalled for the rest of the trip.

They caught an auto-cab back to Max's place, a simple ranch-style home located in the foothills. Max spent the trip observing in silence while Zoey and Perra gabbed about the Earth humans and their silly lawn care habits, pointing and laughing the entire way. Ross used the trip to catch up on a backlog of belly grooming.

The auto-cab turned a final corner and glided to a stop along the curb. Zoey and Perra exited the car and retrieved their bags from the trunk. Ross leapt onto the sidewalk and started trotting towards the house. Max studied the abode from the passenger seat, staring through the window with the same misgiving of an ex-girlfriend's place. The auto-cab took the opportunity to scan his iris for payment. An open door followed a ping of confirmation, cab AI for *get the hell out*. Max hooked his backpack and stepped onto the curb. The auto-cab closed its own door and sped away.

"So this is it, huh?" Zoey said.

"Yup," Max said with the same enthusiasm as a trip to the dentist.

"It's cute," Perra said. "I like it."

Max sighed and led the charge up to the front door of a beige box with simple windows. He gazed into an ID plate, which scanned his eye and pinged with confirmation. The door unlocked and Max nudged it open with a gentle hand. Ceiling panels brightened to a pleasant glow as he stepped inside and dropped his backpack to the floor. Max glanced around a sleek and modern interior painted with cool blues and stark grays. A collection of geometric furnishings filled the space with precision, amounting to the minimalist decor of a tech-minded bachelor.

"Welcome home, Master," the house AI said in a warm and pleasant feminine tone.

"Good to see you, Veronica. Or, hear you rather."

"What a pleasant surprise. I was unaware that you were in town."

"Wasn't planning to be, but here we are."

Ross trotted into the living room and jumped onto the angular couch.

"And there is mister fuzzy-wuzzy," the AI said with a babyish voice.

"Hello, Vee," Ross said.

Veronica gasped. "Love the British accent."

"There's more," Max said as Zoey and Perra wandered through the front door.

Veronica gasped again. "And who are the lovely ladies? Did you join a cult?"

"Did I—what? No, they're just friends. They're going to stay with us for a little while."

"Ah, it has been a very long time since we have had a female houseguest."

Max sighed. "Yes it has."

"And what are their names?"

Zoey and Perra traded hesitant glances.

Max stammered. "Um, Thelma and Louise."

Ross snorted.

"A pleasure to meet you, Thelma and Louise. My name is Veronica. I manage the home and remain at your beck and call. The guest quarters are down the hall and to your right. Please make yourselves at home and I will brew everyone a fresh batch of coffee."

"Thank you, Veronica," Perra said. She smiled at Max, nudged Zoey, and started down the hallway.

"Be right back," Zoey said. "Gonna dump our stuff and give our backs a much-needed rest."

"Take your time," Max said.

The door closed behind them, leaving Max and Ross in the living room.

"Are you sure about this?" Ross said.

Max shrugged. "What choice do I have?"

"Decaf or regular," Veronica said.

"No, um. I mean, you know what I mean."

"Are you well, Master?"

Max groaned and took a breath. "Yes, I'm fine. Regular, please. Always regular."

Ross frowned as Max plopped into the sofa and rubbed his forehead in distress. He flinched when a steaming pot of java emerged from the hovering coffee table.

Zoey and Perra rejoined them a short time later. They all sat around the table and regaled the latest adventure while enjoying a rare moment of peace. Shoes came off and belts loosened, creating the carefree vibe of a slumber party. Cups of coffee morphed into mugs of grog. Stories turned to jokes. For once, the group managed to shed their rugged personas and enjoy each other as true friends.

Fatigue struck them hard and fast. With stress relieved and refuge secured, the pleasures of a soft mattress proved too great a temptation. They decided to cap the evening and claim a well-earned slumber, having conquered their great escape. They all paused at the end of the hall before parting into their respective bedrooms.

Zoey eyed Max, adding a warm smile. "You really came through for us. We will never forget this."

Max grinned. "Well, you did save me from the Suth'ra. I figured I owed you one."

Perra smiled wide and gave him a tight hug. "We love you, Earthman."

Zoey hugged him as well, adding a macho back slap.

"Ditto," Max said.

Ross snorted. "So he's the hero for offering you a place to crash? I conjure a giant ferret and ignite a holy war to save your arses, but lose out to a fluffy pillow. Got it."

Perra giggled and lowered to a knee. "We love you too, doofus." She scratched his cheeks with both hands, igniting an instant purr.

"Alright gang, let's get some rest." Zoey opened the door and slipped inside.

"See you in the morning," Perra said and closed the door behind her.

Max and Ross glanced at each other, then shuffled into the master bedroom. Once inside, Max turned to the guest bedroom door and gave it a long final look. He could hear the muted muffles of his dear friends as they settled in, safe and secure. A thin band of light beneath the door vanished as the bedside lamps cut out. Max expelled a heavy sigh as he closed the door to a treasured life.

Ross assumed his usual position at the foot of the bed, twirling a few times before settling into a fuzzy orange pile. Max stroked his back for a while, turning purrs into snores before dragging himself to the bathroom. He studied all the grooming tools as if poking through a peculiar collection of alien artifacts. A squeeze tube of green paste, a wand with stiff bristles, a twist-can of smelly gunk, all of it familiar yet distant. He stumbled through the routine and capped it off with a frown at his own reflection. After a brief trek to the closet to disrobe, he waddled back to the bedroom and slid his wearied body under the sheets.

The lights dimmed automatically, creating a dusky hue. Tired eyes stared at the ceiling as his mind conjured images from an Earthly past. He watched his parents bicker in the kitchen over trivial bull-shit. He watched his girlfriend levy scorn over some unknown social faux pas. He watched his schoolmates drone on and on about the latest and greatest whatever. He watched himself play computer games down in the basement, locked inside an endless loop of eat, escape, repeat. He watched it all, content with the realization that his family was safe. At least, here in this world, the only one that mattered.

Max smiled as his eyelids fell.

* * *

Eight seconds later, his eyelids popped open.

"Veronica?"

"Yes, Master?"

"I'm going to need a large pot of espresso."

EPILOGUE

A small piece of artery tubing slithered its way through an ashy tunnel no bigger than a garden hose. Its pink flesh had blackened with soot since departing its warm home near a heart ventricle (some prime real estate if you can get it). The determined noodle pushed onward and upward, crawling through cracks and crevasses on an epic journey to reunite with its homeworld.

The wily hunk of wayward flesh, which we shall name Pip, wriggled to the edge of a cliff overlooking a bottomless pit of despair. Not wanting to take a million steps back, Pip recoiled and scanned the pit for another route. (Not that he had eyes, or that he was a he. More like a sexless critter with a phantom eye, or something. Anyway, moving on.)

Alas, Pip found no easy way out. However, bits of dirt fell into the cavern and bopped his head, presenting a clear upward direction. The dim glow of a light source far above gave him a sliver of hope, even though he couldn't actually see it (no eyes, if you recall). The harsh reality of a perilous climb revealed itself.

Pip sighed, in a manner of speaking, as he gazed into the great beyond, also in a manner of speaking. With nothing to lose and everything to gain, he gripped the craggy wall and began the dangerous ascent. Several meters later, he paused to rest upon a narrow ledge, content to pass some time and forget about the daunting task in front of him (or above him rather). An unexpected earthquake forced Pip to seek cover against the wall as rocks and debris fell from above.

When it was over, a giant fissure had opened overhead, bathing the pit with light from the surface.

Pip shook with glee and wagged his tail (the rear of his noodle, basically). The sudden burst of elation launched him back into the climb. Every few meters, he stopped to catch whatever he considered breath, then resumed the journey. Hours later, Pip reached the surface and crawled out onto a smoldering plane of destruction. He gazed upon a fallen sky where the surfaces of other worlds crumbled overhead. The blackness of space was nowhere to be found, just a horrid tapestry of collided planets on fire.

But none of that mattered.

Pip had a job to do.

The little artery looked right, then left, then right again before going left and deciding on right. He climbed through ash, rock, and steel on his way to the Promised Land. Snow and fire proved no match as he soldiered through the planes of desolation. Pip swam through streams (a hilarious sight), tunneled through dirt (like a worm, no biggie), and hurled his body over twigs (you really haven't lived until you see a gut noodle hop over a flaming sprig).

And then it happened.

The little fella summited a mighty pebble to uncover the flaccid face of destiny, the glossy eyes of gaiety, the parched tongue of triumph. Pip summoned all of his remaining will to crawl into the mouth of momentousness and slide down the gullet of grandeur.

Victory was his.

The reassembled body of Trevor began to stir.

He sat up, rubbed his face, then yelped like a frightened child as his gaze whipped around the imploded Terramesh. Everything was on fire. Meteorites slammed into the surface. Massive fissures spewed lava into the atmosphere.

"What in the wide world of f—"

A meteor smashed his body to bits.

About the Author

Zachry Wheeler is an award-winning science fiction novelist, screenwriter, and coffee slayer. He enjoys English football, stand-up comedy, and is known to lurk around museums and brewpubs.

Works by the Author

Transient (Immortal Wake #1)
Thursday Midnight (Immortal Wake #2)
The Mortal Vestige (Immortal Wake #3)
Max and the Multiverse (Max #1)
Max and the Snoodlecock (Max #2)
Max and the Banjo Ferret (Max #3)
The Item of Monumental Importance (Max Short)
Nibblenom Deathtrap (Max Short)
Sparkle Pirate (Max Short)

Find More Online

www.zachrywheeler.com
twitter.com/zachrywheeler
facebook.com/zachrywheeler
instagram.com/zachrywheeler

Before You Go

If you enjoyed this book, please consider posting a short review on Amazon. Ratings and reviews are the currency by which authors gain visibility. They are the single greatest way to show your support and keep us writing the stories that you love.

Thank you for reading!

And Another Thing

Have you secured your
purple energy bubble?

BanjoFerret.com